BEAUTY

Also by Frederick Dillen

Hero
Fool

BEAUTY

a novel

FREDERICK DILLEN

Simon & Schuster

New York   London   Toronto   Sydney   New Delhi

Simon & Schuster
1230 Avenue of the Americas
New York, NY 10020

First Simon & Schuster hardcover edition March 2014

SIMON & SCHUSTER and colophon are registered trademarks of Simon & Schuster, Inc.

For information about special discounts for bulk purchases, please contact Simon & Schuster Special Sales at 1-866-506-1949 or business@simonandschuster.com.

The Simon & Schuster Speakers Bureau can bring authors to your live event. For more information or to book an event contact the Simon & Schuster Speakers Bureau at 1-866-248-3049 or visit our website at www.simonspeakers.com.

Designed by Aline C. Pace

Manufactured in the United States of America

10 9 8 7 6 5 4 3 2 1

Library of Congress Cataloging-in-Publication Data
Dillen, Frederick G., 1946-
  Beauty : a novel / Frederick G. Dillen.
     pages cm
1. Businesswomen—Fiction. 2. Corporations—Massachusetts—Fiction. I. Title.
  PS3554.I415B43 2014
  813'.54—dc23
                                        2013028658

ISBN 978-1-4767-1692-3
ISBN 978-1-4767-1694-7 (ebook)

To Leslie, who begins me and ends me and is joy between.

BEAUTY

Battle Bay

It could have been any factory anywhere. Carol MacLean had been shutting places down for that long. And after all these years, each place hurt more than the last. The good news was that after two more burials, this one and the next, she would finally get her own company, which was everything she could want.

Today was the Battle Bay pulp and paper mill in northern Wisconsin, and after a breath, she went into the lunchroom to deliver her news. She had come expecting to introduce herself and finish this hardest part of things in a couple minutes. Instead she pulled a metal folding chair to the wall behind the men. They couldn't have numbered more than forty, and they didn't begin to fill this lunchroom that had once served several shifts.

At the other end of the room, the owner stood on another folding chair. He wasn't dressed much differently than his men, and he looked at them as if he knew them. There was nothing of practical value he could say, but he had wanted to talk to these last few, which didn't happen all the time, and Carol had thought it was a sympathetic gesture. Then he began with "Here we are," and was already choked up. He cared about his men, but maybe he cared too much. Carol sat forward in her chair.

She was already alert in the usual ways. Once you came through the door, if you didn't project authority, you knew it and the men knew it, and that made everything worse for everybody. She also reached in her pocket to check that her phone was off. When it came time for her to say what she had to say, the men should know they were all that was on her mind.

The owner said, "Most of you knew my father. But my grand-father . . ." The men shifted in their chairs. The owner said, "With your skills and dedication," and made something like a sob.

Carol got up.

The owner said, "Excuse me. It's an emotional day. Those of you still here, we've known one another, worked together, for a long time."

Carol walked to the front of the room.

The owner said in a sorrowful whisper, "I let you down."

Carol reached him and said, "Why don't you let me take over?" He looked confused, and she held up a hand to help him off his chair. He took her hand and stepped down and walked to the door, and Carol climbed up on the chair in his place.

She said to the men, "This is it. You knew it was coming. I wish I could say there might be an emergency-room deal with Baxter Blume, but there won't. These old buildings will be tear-downs when we get what we can get for what's inside. Your owner has promised you, and set aside, two weeks' pay; I'll make sure that you receive it. If you have any problems, you can find me in the offices."

They got up, and when they were up, they stood. They were

the oldest and the last, and they just didn't want to leave yet. Every man she could, she looked in the eye. Her father had been a machinist for a supplier outside Detroit. He had died at his bench because that was who he was and what he did and, finally, all he had besides his four packs a day. To the men here, Carol said, "I'm sorry," and she meant it. In her heart she also said it to her father.

It was out of bounds for Carol to tell herself that she hurt when she closed places down and fired people, but she did, and it felt as if all of the closings and firings had piled up on top of her. One more, and she'd be out from underneath them. Instead of an undertaker she'd be a CEO. All right, she'd be a back-door CEO in some pocket-size outfit, nothing the equity partners at Baxter Blume could ever dream of wanting, but Carol had always dreamed of it.

For now, she still faced the men of Battle Bay. She said, "There's information on the sheets outside, and your union has material for you." She nodded to them and said, "Good luck."

A few at first, and then all of them, turned and left, and Carol got down from her chair.

When she reached in her pants pocket to turn on her cell, it vibrated. Baxter. Neither Baxter nor Blume nor any of the rest of them ever went near a plant floor with bad news. They would not have admitted it, but Carol could tell they were frightened of the workingmen they put out of work. Carol came from workingmen and wasn't frightened. After coming up as a parts salesman for the Best Motor Company, she had what once seemed like the best job she'd ever get, as the lowest of Baxter Blume's executives.

Baxter's joke was to ask how many bodyguards she needed each time she told men their jobs were history. Was it a five-bodyguard event? Five was the high. She played along because, behind the joke, Carol believed Baxter respected what she did, delivering the news, and then the slog of disposal that came afterward. Not that there really were bodyguards today or most days, though in a few places she had gotten people to watch her car for the duration.

Today she said quickly, before Baxter could get into his banter, "The next company after this is the last." As she spoke, Carol remembered the heartbreak in the owner's face and the emptiness in the faces of the men.

Baxter said, "I'm thinking four bodyguards. I can feel it from here." There was laughter in his background.

Carol said, "Baxter, you told me that after my next corporate burial I'm done as an undertaker."

"Five? Tell me you don't need five bodyguards. Do I need to make calls for your safety?"

"One more company to bury, and then I get my own company to run. I need to hear you promise me that again."

"Okay, Carol, okay. The next company is the last one you bury."

"And then I get my own company to run."

"The gears are already turning, Carol, cross my heart."

She said, "I broke the news today without any bodyguards, but you, Baxter, you would have wanted five."

Before she hung up, she heard someone say through the laughter, "Nobody screws with the Beast."

Carol pocketed the phone and took a breath and moved on.

New York

When Baxter saw Carol MacLean walk past his door with a *Journal* under her arm, he was not happy. Fortunately he was on the other side of his office, so she didn't see him. Baxter had bad news for Carol, and he didn't want to break it now, and he hadn't thought he'd have to. Truth be told, he couldn't. Carol was supposed to be on her way up the coast to bury a little fish-processing outfit. After which, he'd tell her.

Baxter watched her stride down the hallway. She was wearing a skirt instead of pants, and high heels that weren't remotely high but were a statement for Carol just the same. Baxter thought he knew what the statement was. She'd come in today to make sure that, after this next burial, she would be getting her company. She wasn't going to say so outright, he hoped. She wouldn't want to press so hard he'd reconsider. Baxter himself wouldn't say what he had to say either.

She looked good, relatively speaking. Whether she was dressed up or not, though, Baxter had always found her a mystifying presence. Really she was nothing but bones and angles and parchment-white skin, so thin you could see through her. She was also, what, six-one, but from a generation of women who didn't want to be tall, which was why she almost never wore high heels. The tall ones now wore heels that put them most of the way to the ceiling, which sometimes Baxter appreciated and sometimes didn't. Anyhow, Carol was flat chested along with everything else, not that Baxter stared at his employees. But what she did have was the great red hair she'd managed to keep all these years. That and posture. She wasn't just erect; despite her natural and professional courtesy, she had always held her shoulders back like a wrong-side-of-the-tracks tough girl. Baxter would never entirely understand it, but taken as a whole, Carol possessed what his mother had always wished he had: character. Baxter liked Carol for it. What's more, he'd known she was ready to run her own company for years now, and that made everything harder. He wished to hell she hadn't come in today. Dressed up, for Christ sake.

He followed her down the hall and stepped into the copy alcove when she stopped at the large conference room, where in fact Baxter was due shortly. Both doors to the conference room were open, and he could see that the room was mostly full. Blume was in and down. Patterson sat in the corner with his numbers acolytes. The numbers wore khakis and no ties. Blume and Patterson, and Baxter, were in suits because they had a prospect on deck later.

Patterson avoided noticing Carol, but Blume turned around, and since Carol wasn't supposed to be in today, Blume's face registered the surprise. Baxter knew Blume would not register the heels and the skirt. Those were for Baxter. Carol dropped her *Journal* on the conference table and walked, shoulders back, toward the wall of windows facing downtown. As she went, she made a little nod to Blume. She'd always thought Blume cared about her career. No foundation in that whatever, Baxter thought. Carol was smart in many ways, but a bit dense politically. Baxter waited to figure out what she was going to do. He hoped she was going to leave and soon. He hated the fact that, by a petty agreement with Blume, he was forbidden to tell her what she deserved to know. Blume. Baxter wanted to tell her regardless, give her a better shot going forward.

Patterson's acolytes watched her, probably wondering. Why wouldn't they wonder? They weren't likely to understand Carol. They were all over twenty-one, but none of them looked eighteen, which was how you looked when you had gone to good schools and were smart and lucky and had not yet gotten your nose rubbed in it like Carol. Of course, to Baxter, everybody looked younger now, which he chose to take as a measure of his own enlarged authority (not the prostate yet after all).

Remy was at the table. He had always been Carol's team and was soon to be more. He had probably looked old the day he was born. He also had all the wrong schools for Baxter Blume. Carol had spotted him six years ago, when he was a doomed intern, and she had asked for him and gotten him. Because Carol was so seldom in town, they relied on each other and, as best Baxter could tell, had become friends.

Susannah was the only other woman in the room. Susannah was someone who made a commitment and took a position on it, a pledger who right now gave all her attention to marking out her territory on the conference room's tabletop. Susannah tailored and displayed herself as young and smart and capable, all true. Blume had been determined to hire Susannah. She would be the first woman to have any equity participation in Baxter Blume.

Carol would never have gotten equity participation, which she'd have long since guessed. Carol, God help her, had always wanted a company anyway.

Carol turned around from the windows, and Baxter moved to watch her through the surprisingly large crack between the alcove door and its frame. Carol looked to Blume, who was not going to look back. Remy, however, smiled up at her from whatever he was running. Carol wouldn't have expected Remy at a meeting like this unless he'd told her about it ahead of time, which he had been forbidden to do. If Carol was startled to see him, however, she barely showed it. She smiled at one of the numbers who had freckles and red hair. Nice-looking kid who had no idea that Carol, alas, thought her own company was almost in reach.

But Carol wasn't leaving anytime soon, and Baxter had to run this meeting. He stepped out around his door, and as he did, Carol started to move as if she was in fact going to leave. Too late. Everybody'd seen him. She'd seen him. She froze.

"Carol," he said as he made his entrance, taking in all of his kingdom.

She stood waiting for him to zero in on her.

"Carol," he said again, and sat down across the table from her. He wondered if she was nervous. She didn't show nervous. Coming up blue collar, with nothing but an undergraduate business degree from a vo-tech school, she would've had to learn about a whole different order of thick skin. On the other hand, business was apparently all she'd ever wanted from the time she was four or five. Was that what she'd said? Helping delinquents in her neighborhood alley manage expenses while they made hot rods of the cars they'd stolen. All right, the "stolen" part was Baxter's gift to a story Carol had only told once.

He let her stand there, frozen. He said, to everyone but her, "Why is Carol MacLean here?" Baxter went with full names for problems. Carol would long since have learned that. What an asshole he was. Exactly the point.

He asked his kingdom, "Shouldn't Carol MacLean be out somewhere hitting something over the head? Shouldn't she be digging a hole to bury the carcass?"

Believe it or not, he was doing Carol a favor. He turned back to her and said, "Get lost, Carol. Beasts do not belong in Baxter Blume's offices." To her credit, in Baxter's opinion, she showed nothing.

This was ugly behavior even for Baxter. He only ground on people when they needed grinding, but Carol hadn't needed grinding for years. Besides which, he was the one guy who never called her the Beast. He trusted she would put the pieces together. They'd scheduled a meeting when she was supposed to be on the road; they'd invited Remy to the table on his own account; Baxter himself was being, even for him, a superhuman asshole. Baxter watched Carol check the boxes.

Baxter Blume put together buyouts of two-hundred-, three-hundred-, four-hundred-million-dollar targets that had accumulated extraneous divisions. The viable divisions got reconfigured or set aside for later, and the rest got loaded with debt and Carol buried them. Which was not how she got nicknamed the Beast, but by now a lot of numbers had come and gone thinking it was, that and being tall and pale and bony and with the crazy hair not everybody admired as much as Baxter. And that spoke to the problem. Baxter was taking a break from things, or from the next fund anyway. That meant he wouldn't be around to wave Carol's flag, and that meant the people who didn't get Carol could get rid of her. They could have Remy to take over the burials at a lower salary than

Carol now commanded. Baxter was no longer sure that he could get Carol the company that she deserved and that he'd promised even if he was full speed around the office.

Carol smiled at Baxter. Baxter was relieved. She had received the message. Good for you, Carol, he thought. Not only did she know she was out, she was taking it like a soldier.

Carol was on her way to Massachusetts for her last burial. There would be time for her to line up a new position. Baxter would help her with that, if she ever chose to speak to him again. What's more, Baxter knew she would do a good job on her last burial. That was Blume's concern, that if Carol knew she was out, she'd bail on this last job, which was a horseshit concern if you knew Carol.

She walked back around the table, and when she got behind Baxter, she put the heel of her hand on his shoulder and held him down as he pretended he was going to stand.

She said, "Don't try to get up, Baxter. We all know that's gotten difficult for you." And she walked from the room.

Shit, Baxter thought. If Carol understood she was out, she would know to forgo the sarcasm and concentrate on the recommendations she was going to need. Had she thought he was giving her a final exam on toughness before turning her company over to her? And was she letting him know that she was immune to any ugliness he could muster? She was dialed into her company and standing up for it. Baxter had not gotten the message across after all. He opened his mouth to say something, but what could he say?

The khaki number with freckles whispered loudly enough for her to hear, "Beast." And before Baxter could tell him to shut up, everybody else, including Blume and Patterson, whispered loudly in chorus, well before she could have gotten past reception and out the lobby doors, "Beast, Beast, Beast."

Salvage

She was in the car on the Mass Pike, still trying to figure what had put Baxter into his asshole mood. She thought maybe there was something up with the fish plant. That would explain why they'd brought Remy in. Carol had just happened to walk across the line of fire. She could take it, and she had years of practice shrugging off the Beast stuff, though Baxter had never thrown it at her before. His hair was seriously on fire, about the fish outfit and a lot more. Her phone went off, and she tried to come up with what he needed to be told.

"Carol." It was Remy in his keep-calm, bus-wreck voice.

She said, "Let me call you back." So she didn't have to deal with Baxter right now.

If it was Remy, there was a problem at the fish plant, but how bad could it be? Remy's bus-wreck voice meant there could be news of an executive at the plant who carried automatic weapons and was off his medication. Or a workforce of amputees. Worst case, Baxter had suddenly decided Carol had zero time in which to clean house and run the garage sale. Whatever it was, she had seen it before and could handle it.

All that actually counted was what always counted: the fish plant, in this case, didn't fit with anything Baxter Blume had in hand or in the pipeline and was not viable on its own. Carol's background this time around was thinner than usual, but the basics were familiar. Baxter Blume had had to take the fish plant along with a package of more appealing components acquired from a Japanese firm. The Japanese had gotten the plant from Germans, the initial outside owners of what had for generations been a private company under local ownership. The Germans had made a mistake and talked the Japanese, supposedly a more natural fish owner, into making another mistake. For Baxter Blume, the fish plant was simply a cheap lubricant to get the Japanese deal out the door. As best Carol could tell, there had once been enough profits to justify a loan for a new plant even as the margins were shrinking. Now, with the North Atlantic fish stock apparently approaching terminal depletion, the fish-processing industry had itself reached a stasis of consolidation that left Carol's near corpse of the moment not only far too small to compete but also deeply in debt.

The comforting thing was that the officers of the plant, all but one with the company for decades, had stayed through the corporate changes. These had been the local owners, and presumably they would have had a chance to pull out with both the Germans and the Japanese. Which told Carol that the owner-executives, and all the line workers, too (neighbors after all), might have a sentimental interest in keeping the company on an even keel as she dismantled and disposed. There were valuable physical assets, and she believed she could keep processing frozen fish, of which there seemed to be a fair amount, as she negotiated the sales of the lines and whatever else. It wouldn't hurt to be able to tell buyers that the lines were operating. It wouldn't hurt the locals to pocket a few more paychecks before the final severance.

Carol could hardly believe this was her last burial. As she said that to herself again, something clicked into place. Baxter's noise in the conference room had been his way of showing everybody that, after all her years as an undertaker, Carol was tough enough to take the heat as a CEO.

Pine and fir began to green the roadside woods, and the sun was out, so she got off the freeway to drive the two-lane roads. She drove east and a bit north, as best she could determine. She drove without the clutch for the fun of it.

When she crossed the short bridge over the channel that made Elizabeth Island, she saw signs to the industrial park, which was not big but which was real enough to look familiar. It had an engineering group and a circle with medical offices; it had professionals and contractors and somebody's little tech component division. It had the new plant for Elizabeth's Fish and its latest corporate mask, Elizabeth Seafood Products.

Carol drove past the corporate offices and the executive parking. She drove around behind the plant itself, which was a good-size box.

Here was a two-hundred-year-old company, originally a family company, with brand-new parking for at least a hundred cars, all the lines still bright and white on uncracked asphalt after a first winter, the earth still raw where the edges met the woods and where the snow was gone except for the plow leavings. It was very nice and very ample parking for a very shiny new plant that Carol knew had state-of-the-art equipment, from its processing lines to its wrap-and-stack to its cold facilities, which included some tricky automated truck-to-freezer cold receiving and pallet-to-truck cold load. It was a new turnkey plant with great employee parking.

And twenty cars in the lot. More parking lot than employees. More building than employees.

Carol would have expected the plant to have lost a shift or two, but she had also assumed there would be a sizable workforce to keep the place generating the profits, however meager, it was declaring. Whatever their respective faults, the Germans and Japanese were not likely to have been knowing stewards of a completely fraudulent factory. They would both, however, have relied on the operational reports from the local management.

Carol came to any burial with questions. This time she had more than usual because Baxter Blume had bought the company so cheaply and so quickly that due diligence had gone out the window. But Carol's strength, "her meal ticket," as Baxter liked to say so frequently, was her "knee-jerk" sense of things. That was Baxter's way of saying that it didn't matter if Carol couldn't read a sophisticated balance sheet because at the undertaker level of things, common sense was more useful.

What was her knee-jerk here?

On the map, Elizabeth Island was a small fist of land that pushed out of far northeast Massachusetts into the Atlantic. It had a harbor that used to support a substantial fishing industry, but that industry had been declining for more than twenty years and had been all but gone for at least five.

Yet here was a brand-new, state-of-the-art fish plant, in the woods no less, all but idle.

Carol would have to bury the company no matter what, but she'd want to get senior management away from the cash register in the next ten or fifteen minutes.

She circled back to the front, where the executive parking lot was sparsely but expensively stocked and where six landscape guys with a flatbed and a pickup and a mini-backhoe were getting the Elizabeth Seafood Products (ESP) public grounds ready for spring sod.

And here came—who? The president of ESP? She thought so. Another call came in from Remy, but she didn't answer. She was into it now, whatever the problem might be. She took her time getting out of the car and putting on her jacket, and she locked the car before facing the president. She let him come to her.

She smiled and walked a few steps to meet the president, to show him some respect, to honor the fact that he'd come out in shirtsleeves on a cold afternoon.

"Carol," he said in a good imitation of a down-market Baxter, and they met beside a midsize Mercedes. Maybe it was his Mercedes, and maybe, Carol thought, that made him feel okay. He smiled and held out his hand.

She shook it and said, "Mr. Mathews?"

"Pete, please. We didn't think we'd see you until tomorrow, but I've had my assistant keeping an eye out the window for prowlers. Nice little vehicle you have. How do you like the looks of our new home? Come on inside. It's the end of the day, but you can take a peek and meet some of us. We're eager as can be about the new association with Baxter Blume."

She let him take her elbow and guide her at the grand entrance to ESP, but after a few steps, she pointed over at the landscapers.

He stopped. "Getting ready to decorate with some sod. A frill, maybe, but at not much expense, and I've found it makes a difference in morale and in relationships. May I call you Carol?"

She said, "Why don't we send them home?" He flinched, and covered it.

"They're almost on their way right now. They usually break at four thirty. Come on inside so the team doesn't have to squint through the blinds to check you out." Mathews chuckled.

"Let's send them home for good, Mathews."

"Yep. Fair enough. You've found a soft spot in your first five minutes, Carol, but I think it's the only one you're going to find. We've always run a tight ship here, no pun intended, and we've been able to tighten up considerably since the Japanese ownership began pulling back. We can talk to you about that for the rest of the afternoon and all day tomorrow. I'll get my assistant to send out the facilities guy and we'll go to gravel and be the better for it. I think we're all going to be on the same page in this thing, Carol, and we're going to benefit from your good eye. Costs. Yep, there will be things we've overlooked in the forest because we're too close to the trees. But not many, I think you'll find."

Carol stood her ground and watched him talk. He knew. She said, "Let's you and I go right now and get it over with." She pried his hand off her elbow and took hold of his elbow. "Come on," she said and pulled him toward the landscapers' trucks. "Hold on a minute, men," she called.

The foreman waited for them by the door of the flatbed.

"Marco," Mathews said. "We're going to go with the gravel. I know we talked about sod and you've been getting ready for the sod, but we're cutting back all over and we've decided to pull back out here as well. I'll have somebody call your office and work it out first thing in the morning. The gravel is going to look fine with everything else you've already done. Okay? Thank you, Marco, and excuse us. We've got a lot on our plate."

Mathews started away, but Carol held him where he was. She said to Marco, who was not yet able to read things clearly, "No gravel. Nothing. You're done here. Any charges will need to be thoroughly detailed. I have to tell you we'll be looking closely and arguing wherever we can."

"Mr. Mathews?" Marco said. He was figuring it out now, at one level or another.

Mathews had turned most of the way back around toward the building, but she still had his elbow. She gave him a squeeze, and he looked back at Marco and nodded and said, "Let's leave it at that, Marco. That makes the best sense. Let's just shut it down for now."

Marco might have been sorry to lose his contract, but he looked glad to see Mathews take it in the shorts. Once in a while when the Beast was on duty, people could be glad. Carol said, "Let's go meet the team, shall we?"

λ

They went into the executive offices, and Mathews gave Carol a quick look down into the plant from the second floor. Carol didn't know fish from flamingos, but she saw what had to be six lines and everything necessary to support a three-shift operation. She wondered if she was going to be able to find a buyer to take all of it. Wouldn't that be nice? Mathews wanted to talk, and she paid no attention and he shut up. He'd done all his kidding outside. Five of his lines were quiet, and obviously there wouldn't be other shifts. Even with the limited information she had, she could connect plenty of dots.

As she and Mathews walked to his suite at the end of the hall, the other guys appeared out of their office doors and fell in behind. There were times when it was sad with the officers, when you knew they were doing their best and doing, all things considered, not a bad job. There were also other times. There were always surprises.

Some of the surprises could be chalked up to the turnovers in ownership. The Germans were a packaging outfit, and they

packaged foods among other things. They were coming unrav-
eled, and this was where it became guesswork for Carol. There
wasn't enough due diligence. So although she wasn't clear on
the time line or how ESP came to their attention, the Germans
seemed to have noticed and appreciated the little bit of cash
reserves that the fish company had at the time. Carol guessed
that, as the German unraveling picked up speed, somebody at
Elizabeth's Fish, Mathews presumably, persuaded somebody in
Bremen that those slight cash reserves could be leveraged into a
new plant that would yield significant positive cash flow. How
would he have made that persuasion? Leaving aside the shrinkage
of groundfish stocks in the ocean, Elizabeth's Fish must have long
been suffering from margin shrinkage in a competition with
much larger fish processors. Soon its cash reserves were going
to be needed just to keep the business afloat. Carol imagined
Mathews coming up against the wall and realizing the Germans
themselves were fractured enough to grab at straws. Let's build
a new plant. Who cares if it won't be large enough to go against
industry leaders? Those reserves, and the dollars they leveraged,
could be channeled through grateful pockets as opposed to a
sinkhole operation. It must have been a surprise when the Japanese took over the company, however briefly. The Japanese knew
fish, but they may have also, as Baxter Blume did, simply taken
Elizabeth's Fish off the Germans' hands in order to close on an
acquisition of other divisions.

Surprise: Mathews had a very nice office.

He offered Carol the low sofa, but she went and stood behind
his desk and watched the rest of the fat boys file in. Mathews
introduced the financial officer, the production manager, and the
sales and marketing guy. If there was an HR guy, he was missing.
Carol didn't speak. She looked at each one in turn, and they sat.

All of them knew she was there to pull the plug on the company. Mathews's pretense aside, they were ready. They'd set themselves up comfortably. They were a foursome for the golf course.

Carol sat in the president's chair and still said nothing. CFO and Production looked at the silenced Mathews and said nothing themselves. Sales and Marketing tried on his smile and leaned forward with an elbow on one knee, then thought better of it. Carol had long since learned that silence worked better than inviting nervous, assertive executive bullshit. Mathews looked out the window at the Mercedes he got to keep and the sod he hadn't quite got placed.

A sequence of quick banters signaled someone coming down the hall toward the open door. That would be Human Resources, and apparently he had a word for every assistant in every open door. Either he was a jerk or they liked him. Neither of which made him honest, but if Carol had to keep one of these guys around, he might be the one. He was the one officer who had not been with the company forever, which could put him outside the golf foursome in ways that would be helpful to her.

He came in, checked out his colleagues sitting on their hands like felons, and walked across the room to her, smiled, and said, "You must be Carol MacLean. I'm Dave Parks. You've figured out I'm HR. Sorry to hold you up. Somebody has a medical insurance emergency."

He had his hand out to shake, and when she didn't look at it, he put it in his pocket.

"Okay," he said. "No talking. I get it," but he looked her in the eye and kept a pleasant smile as he sat down among the others.

When he was down and the smile was gone, Carol stood and said, "We're going to get some packing boxes, and then we're all going to go together to each of your offices so you can gather your belongings and leave the property. Computers stay. If your car is a company lease, call a taxi."

Elizabeth Island was not corporate heartland, and Elizabeth's Fish was a corporate minnow, but these were still grown men at the top of the local pile. Wherever the golf course was, they belonged, and most of them had to have second homes and boats. Even so, it was only Production who stood up indignant. Then Mathews stood because he had to. Sales and Marketing spread his arms and made an incredulous face and stayed down. Hard to figure HR, though he stayed down, too. The chief financial officer looked ready to curl up in a ball.

Production said, "What the hell are you talking about?" and managed to say it like he meant it.

This was one of many times when the Beast thing worked for her. She wasn't taller than he was, but she was as tall, and she said quietly, "Everybody sit down, and I'll remind you what I'm talking about. The short version."

Production put his hands on his hips and stared at her, and she stood still and straight and watched him.

Mathews sat, and Production sat.

Since she lacked necessary background, Carol would have to bullshit now. But it wouldn't have been hard to read this group even if you'd just wandered in out of the rain.

She said, "As soon as the German group started to come apart, you found someone under the radar there to okay your plant and help you leverage your reserves. You moved that money through local real estate interests and local builders and local landscapers and local anybody else with an understanding of happy billing. Your salaries rose to match the prestige of ESP and your new facility. When you needed more money, you borrowed more, enough finally that Baxter Blume probably can't pile any new debt on the company. None of which addresses the hardware in the plant; when I tackle the reselling of all that new equipment, I won't be surprised to find verifiable evidence of sweetheart markups, which could be an easy prosecution. You've put up a perfectly useless plant under the noses of distracted Germans but Germans just the same. Which means you did things carefully. All told, a fair amount of money disappeared into your pockets, but it isn't going to be worth filing charges unless there are flags. Since you guys are smarter than I am, and you knew the territory, there probably won't be flags. For now, I only want to get you out of the building and then check to be sure all your private cash flow spigots have been shut off. If anybody has anything to say about that, I will begin investigations in order to prosecute. Let's do HR's office last."

They helped each other gather and sort, packing one another's souvenir hats and portrait photographs. Carol watched the packing and watched Parks.

When they got to Human Resources, to Parks, she asked him to hold up on the packing and wait in his office for her while she walked the rest of them downstairs and out. The offices wing was not big, and it was mostly emptied for the end of the day. The line workers from the plant were long gone. But there were a few people in the executive parking lot to watch the parade.

Once she had them out the door, Carol watched from inside the lobby with its shimmering fish wallpaper and its sepia blowups of historic waterfront scenes. The CFO was bent over with fear, but the other three held their heads high and walked to their cars with a little bounce, Mathews a big bounce, not only as if he'd figured this would happen and didn't care, but as if they still had good things coming to them. Somewhere inside the company, they had definitely left a few spigots open for themselves.

The Ghosts of Fish

Dave Parks watched out his window as the guys drove away. Maybe Mathews was as glad as he said he was, just to finally have it over. It could also be that he and the other guys had something extra working. Dave didn't want to know about that. He hadn't wanted to stay on when plans for a ridiculous new plant surfaced, already in an advanced stage, but they offered him straight salary for what everybody sensed was a few more years. It was enough to pad the nut for the rest of his life, and he took it. He did an honest day's work, and it let his wife, Barbara, continue to comfortably run her nice little diet center—nice because it brought in pocket money for her and comfortable because she didn't feel she had to do it, something she might have felt if he hadn't taken his extra years.

Carol MacLean wouldn't know anything about that, but she had figured that he was the outsider on the executive team. That had to be why she wanted him to stay behind, to help her shut things down honestly. Not something to jump up and down about, but a few more months of salary wouldn't hurt, and he

said, "Trust me," and she laughed. Definitely a good sign. Mary Wells came on the radio, and he looked for a reaction.

Carol said, "I'm from Detroit."

He said, "Pittsburgh and Detroit. Steel to wheels. Where do we start?"

"Those other four have something else still working, and I'd like to shut it off. Can you help me there?"

"If you're asking whether I have something working myself, the answer is no. I don't have any part in anything working, and never have. To your actual question, our second in command in Finance is a straight arrow, and she's been in the company a long time. She could plug leaks, and she'd know places to look that I don't. Annette Novato. So far, all I've heard her mention is missing electricity."

Carol said, "You stayed out of it."

"I'm here. But I stayed out of it. I did my job. I'll call Annette and have her lock up the checks."

"Are you going home after that?"

Which Dave took to mean that Carol planned on working late and wanted him to sign up. What the hell? "I could stay," he said. "It's Motown night on the radio. We can order in. It's not the city—people go home when the bell rings, so we'll have the building to ourselves. You want me to see if I can get Annette to come back?"

Dave thought he liked Carol. She was to the point, seemed to know what she was doing and did it, had a sense of humor, knew Motown.

She said, "No, but would you lead me through town to the old plant on the harbor? It's still listed in the assets."

Yep, working late to check out a not-exactly-decrepit fish-processing plant, especially after a five-hour drive and a quickdraw boardroom massacre—in Dave's book, that counted, earning your keep.

"It still has the old lines in place. I can get you keys."

"It still has the old lines?"

"It has everything. It has the ghosts of fish."

Too Old a Zebra

It was dark when Carol followed Parks down through the heart of town to the harbor. Elizabeth's Fish took up most of a little spit of land that reached into the harbor, and even in the dark she could tell that an original building had been expanded and connected and connected again to other once-separate buildings along the water. Those would have been the growth decades in the business, when the generations of the family that really built Elizabeth's Fish were smarter and more ruthless than anybody else and had the added benefit of an ocean full of fish.

There were broken security lights, a section of Cyclone fence falling off its poles; Keep Out signs had their first graffiti; in places, the asphalt underfoot was broken to gravel.

Parks said, "Shut a plant, and next day it's Halloween." He said it offhand, but he didn't sound happy.

With the shadows and the night, with the added emptiness of water out beyond the building, the plant would have felt big to someone who wasn't accustomed, but Carol had been around bigger operations.

By the splashes of light from the working security poles, she could see that the biggest investment for some time had been in the façade. The respectable generations would have said, Let's make the place look respectable. After that, every several years, as the amounts of fish and cash flow subsided, it would have been a matter of choosing new colors for the repaintings and then slapping up a new version of the old logo. Carol might be able to find evidence of the German tenure, but probably not the Japanese. The Japanese were selling even as they bought.

"Go home," she said to Parks. "I'm just looking."

"I'm fine," he said. "This is a cemetery that matters. I worked here. Met my second wife here."

"You liked it."

"I don't know liked. I was still young enough to make a go of it, but it wasn't easy at first."

"After Pittsburgh."

"After Pittsburgh. I left things in Pittsburgh. Didn't you ever have an 'after Detroit,' Carol?"

Dividing the blocks in her neighborhood, the "village," people called it, were alleys behind the houses. It was a clean neighborhood in those days, but the houses were small and the lots narrow. The brick of the storefronts in the village was stamped tar paper. In the alley behind her and her father's house, boys met to work on motorbikes and then motorcycles and then cars. They had a garage that could hold one car at a time. Carol found those boys and hung around when she was so much younger that they couldn't even hate her for being a girl. Over the years she learned about motors and then everything to do with cars. When she was still much too young, she made runs to the parts store for the boys. After a while, the parts store guys gave her a little something, and the boys gave her a little something. When she was older, she realized that was business, and she knew she liked business. When she was older still, she realized she would fall in love with one of these boys.

She didn't need to call up any of that, least of all Dominic. She said, mostly to herself, "I never had any befores."

Parks, a good guy, said gently, "That sounds like a song, Carol." Then he laughed and said, "I wish I'd never had any."

Carol nodded to be polite. She hardly ever thought about Dominic. When she did, she ached like she was missing everything. Right now, however, she was looking at her last burial, and after that, no, she was not going to get everything, but she was going to get what she was allowed to want: her own company. She wanted that a lot.

She said to Parks, "So the lines are still inside?"

"If you wanted a fish stick, we could go in right now, pull out a block of frozen, saw off a shingle, run that through the piece cutters and onto the shake pans as the belts move the patties under the oil spray and then the breading sifters. On through the ovens. Are you hungry, Carol? Do you mind me calling you Carol? I'm fine with Ms. MacLean if you prefer."

"I'm not hungry, but I am glad to get an idea of how the line travels. And yes, thank you, please call me Carol."

What she almost said, and decided not to say, was "Please call me Carol instead of Beast." What her own guys, Baxter especially, had said out loud in the conference room in New York, that had stung more than usual. But she needed to focus on business, period. She sure as hell couldn't afford to get distracted and give Baxter a last-minute reason to renege on his promise. She was so close to getting her own company that, just now, here in the dark in front of Elizabeth's Fish, feelings that she'd shut up and forgotten seemed bursting to get out. She was full of her dad raising her alone and her looking out for him like she looked out for the boys in the alley, and then learning to do business the same way, looking out for everybody at Baxter Blume, and doing it as the Beast. And this was the Beast's last appearance. She wanted to hold her breath until she had her company, and then with her first free breath, then she'd smile, and the Beast would be gone.

Parks startled her to attention. "And in the new plant, the lines are shinier and have bells and whistles."

"But it's basically the same line in both plants, right? Fish sticks are fish sticks?"

Parks nodded and said, "Fish sticks are fish sticks."

Carol said, "I'm going to stand here for a while by myself, get this perspective on the new plant. Why don't you head home? We'll map things out in the morning."

Parks handed her a ball of keys and drove off, and Carol was glad to be alone. Parks seemed a straight-ahead guy, and she liked him. She thought she trusted him. He had flipped a switch on the past, but that wasn't his fault. The switch had been there. Dominic was always there if she let him be there. She switched herself back into focus.

Now that her eyes were more accustomed, she spotted a gap in the plant's façade. She saw that the fencing had been bent up enough for someone to slide under. She lay down on her back, reached under, and got a grip on the fence from the other side. She pulled herself through until she could stand. She was in a tunnel of darkness between two of the buildings.

She walked toward a pale glow of lights and what she thought would be the harbor. At the end of the tunnel, water spread from beneath the edge of the dock she stood on. The lights of town stacked up the hill to the left. A dozen small working boats, docked one to another, floated beyond the pier. One fair-size boat on the other side of the harbor had serious, blue-bright lights shining down to the machined clutter of its deck.

Carol didn't know fishing, but she knew the feel of living business, and there was hardly a pulse here, which she half loved. And not because a pulse going away meant a job. The deserted plants and factories had always been sadly beautiful to her, museums of echoes and iron.

Someone came out on the deck of the lighted vessel across the way, and she could hear him talking to someone else inside the boat. The water carried the sound to where she stood. She couldn't make out what he was saying, but he spoke slowly enough that his words, whatever they were, came singsong.

She walked back through the tunnel to the security lights and pulled herself under the fence again. She swiped sand off the back of her suit and got in her car and dialed Remy.

She would find out what he had been doing at the meeting, what he'd learned about her company, what the problem was earlier in the day when she'd been trying to bring her focus together for this one last burial.

Remy picked up and said, "Listen, Carol."

Carol was not somebody who ordinarily needed reassurance, but she had needed it just now, and she liked hearing Remy's voice and imagining him at his desk in New York. She could manage to bury one more body, for God sake. No sweat, as Baxter liked to say. Now she waited for Remy's actual news.

When he didn't say anything, she said, "What?"

Remy said, "Baxter was trying to give you a heads-up with his 'Beast' and his you-don't-belong-here. Because Blume is pushing you out. It's done."

She wasn't hearing this right, and she didn't believe it.

She said, "No." But she'd been afraid of it since before Battle Bay, almost since Baxter first proposed giving her a company to run.

"You're out, Carol. It's done."

"Baxter's unloading me?" He was, and now, when it was already done, her stomach knotted with fear, as if the possibility was just ahead.

"Blume, but yes."

"Blume?" Oh, Jesus. What had she done wrong? Nothing.

"He wanted Susannah to babysit the stand-alone division they're picking up, the one you were supposed to get. It's a little bigger than they thought. Blume got cold feet about giving it to you. He thought you were too old a zebra to get bigger stripes was the way he put it."

Carol sat in her car and felt her company being pulled out of her belly. It felt horrible, and it felt right, as if it was what she'd asked for.

Remy said, "I'm sorry."

"This means I'm an undertaker for life."

"No, Carol."

"I thought Baxter was testing me with the 'Beast' and all his bullshit about belonging in the room. I was sure that if I stood up to it, I was home. Blume looked at me like it was any other day. Did I fuck up?"

"Carol, you're not an undertaker anymore, not for Baxter Blume. Or you won't be as soon as you finish out the fish."

Carol had always had more time being alone than she'd known what to do with. She'd been so alone that she worked harder than anybody else, which it turned out she had to do to get where everybody else got. She'd worked her whole life for this, from the alley, from selling parts and from answering engine fixes over the phone, to killing other people's companies and looking in the eyes of the poor bastards she canned. Everything she'd done, she'd done to have a company she could run herself. She didn't know how she could have worked harder. She didn't know if she could work harder now. She had lived on the road, one burial after another. She had rights to a small interchangeable timeshare apartment in a New York building of flexible corporate time-shares; when she was there, she put out the few pictures she had. Her company was going to be the place where she would stop and stay.

"They plan to break the news when the fish company is off the books. Baxter figured you could use the early warning to start looking. You know a lot of people, Carol."

"They think somebody else can do it cheaper. Baxter thinks once I hear about my company going to Susannah, I won't perform. Blume knows better than that."

"It's Blume."

"I'm somebody unusual in the firm, but what the hell, I've been unusual for years."

"Baxter likes you. But he's taking less of a role in the new fund, which leaves Blume in charge and you hanging."

"And you're the guy who can do it cheaper. Not that anybody cares about cheaper."

"I'm sorry, Carol. If I didn't take it, they would have got somebody else."

She could tell from his voice that he was sorry. "It's not your fault, Remy. I just didn't know it would be like this."

He said, "Carol?"

She said, "If I'm going to bury this fish, I have to go. Thank you."

She closed her phone and could barely breathe.

She stood up out of the car and made herself breathe deeply. She was fine. There was nothing Carol MacLean couldn't handle.

Then before she knew it, Carol MacLean was on her hands and knees in the blown sand that surrounded the last body she was supposed to bury. She was the healthiest businessman she knew, and she was on her hands and knees and sobbing so hard she couldn't get up. Thank God Parks from HR had gone, though if he'd stayed she'd never have let herself. The sobs became gasping heaves, as if she could weep herself to death. When finally the sobs let go of her, she rocked forward and backward, knees to hands to knees to hands, until her bones were numb on the sanded asphalt.

Oh, Jesus. The lights of a car. Parks was coming back.

The thing was to pretend she had fallen.

She didn't look at the sound of the car door and the first footsteps. It was a truck door. So, not Parks. She got her breath and she composed her face. If she'd fallen, her face could show that she was sore somewhere. She got her voice ready to work.

Beat-up work boots and jeans.

"Are you all right?" someone said.

She was so relieved it wasn't Dave Parks that she could have put her forehead down against the asphalt and sand.

Whoever it was said, "I have a fishing boat docked across the harbor, and I saw the lights here. Thought I'd check it out."

By now, Carol was Carol. She could have gotten up, and she would get up. This was a man with a nice voice. Instead of getting up, she said, "Thank you."

A boot stepped closer, a serious boot but too close, and a hand took hold of her arm.

"I can get up." Her voice was not nice.

Though she didn't mind the hand. She could see it was a strong, callused hand, around her arm just under her armpit. The best place to hold if you're picking anybody up. It felt like she hadn't been touched in years.

He said, "I know you can get up, but around here, especially men like me, we don't get much chance to practice as gentlemen. Don't be angry." But she was up before he was through with his speaking.

She started to tip over, but she didn't fall because the man's hand on her arm tightened enough to keep her steady, and with his other hand, he brushed free the strands of her hair that were caught in his grip on her arm.

Carol smiled at this man, who she realized was shorter than she was. She had lost her company before she got it, so if she was ever going to become somebody who smiled, she would have to start it on her own. She had money, not a lot, nothing like the equity players at Baxter Blume, but enough. She'd been down on her hands and knees so completely that she was unsteady even with his hand firm on her arm.

She said, "I'm . . ." and then she wasn't standing. There was no *kind of* fainting. It was just an elevator down, because she was disoriented from how hard she had sobbed.

He knelt beside her and helped her to sit. His other hand, which had brushed her hair, was now across in front of her, holding her other shoulder.

He let go of her shoulder but kept hold of her arm and said, "Are you okay?" He said it half like a joke, since how okay could she be at the moment?

She tried to smile. She did smile. She said, "I will be. I tripped and fell." Then instead of him saying something when it was his turn, he just looked at her. He had kind eyes. She said, "I got a very hard telephone call and it knocked me down."

He stopped smiling and said, "I'm sorry," but he did not stop looking at her.

Two things. First, she never spoke like that to anyone, hard-call-knocked-me-down. Second, in the business of her life, if you broke your arm or had appendicitis, everybody ran to help you and get you to the hospital and came and checked on you, but if you said out loud that your heart was broken over a terrible disappointment, then people backed off.

This man kept looking at her. He said, "I'm Ezekiel Parsons, and you're Carol MacLean, and if there's anything I can do to make you feel better, tell me. I have my harmonica with me."

She didn't know about harmonicas, but she knew this was a small town. A lot of people would know her name by now. She pointed back at the old plant and was all ready to admit to being the Beast. But she didn't. She just smiled. He smiled again, too. Ezekiel Parsons. She nodded at him and he helped her get up again and she realized how dark it was. They were lit only by a couple security lights along the fencing around the old plant.

He looked her up and down, and before she understood he was still trying to be sure she was all right, she was wishing she had a chest to push out.

"Okay," she said.

"Okay," he said and looked unsure of what they were talking about. She was glad she wasn't the only one who didn't know.

"Thank you for stopping," she said. "I needed your hand getting up." Then she said, "I have to make one more call from the car. This one is an okay call. I'll be fine." She sat in her car to fake it.

His eyes let go of hers, and he was already going away.

She said, "Ezekiel Parsons."

He said, "Carol MacLean," as he sat into his truck. He waved, his other hand already on the steering wheel and drove off. She hadn't even heard his engine start.

When he and his lights were altogether gone, she walked to the fence and stood with her fingers through the chain links. Out the tunnel to the dock and the harbor, she could see the lights from his boat and then she couldn't see them. She had lost her company. She held on to the fence so the punch in her stomach would not bring her to her knees all over again.

Easy Parsons

Parsons had seen the lights at the old plant and wondered whether it was the woman, that the secretaries at the company had said was coming to check on the old plant before deep-sixing it. Jesus, but that was a depressing thought, even if Mathews and his gang were such assholes.

He was right. It had been her. What he hadn't expected was to find her on her knees, her face wet from crying. The secretaries said that supposedly she was called "the Beast" by her colleagues, and now of course Matthews and the rest. If you had half a brain you would look at Carol MacLean, anytime, anywhere, and know the thing about the Beast was just some cruel bullshit. You also knew, when you found her the way Easy found her, that she was a tough woman. As soon as he showed up, she stood and fell back down and stood again and pretended right through it.

She also admitted her hurt about as briefly as possible. Hard call that knocked her down. Six words. And no matter how brief, Easy saw the hurt.

The people around Easy, when he was still there in Mississippi, they'd seen his hurt. Of course some of them didn't mind him hurting. He'd been from somewhere else and he'd loved too much and he hadn't minded saying two words, ugly words about what he thought of God for letting his wife and baby die. He couldn't have been happier when everybody left him alone, except his friend, Rice, who couldn't bear to see somebody need as bad as Easy had needed. What Easy had needed was the love that was gone, so Rice had given him a harmonica and taught him how to play.

Whatever had put Carol MacLean to her knees, Easy believed she needed something. He didn't imagine her the harmonica type, but he was glad he'd at least showed up to be a friend. Also, for a woman out in the storm, she'd looked nice. He'd have wanted to help anyhow, but no argument, she was a good-looking woman.

Easy parked the truck and went on board the boat and belowdecks and to bed.

Women

Either Carol could hold on to the fence forever or, as her father would tell her, pull her damn socks up. She let go of the fence and stood on her own two feet like she was as tough as the next jerk. She got back in her car and drove the streets of Elizabeth Island, looking for the furnished unit that would be her home for the next few weeks.

She found the place. She always found the place. It was at one end of downtown Elizabeth. It wasn't a motel. It belonged to the company and had housed the executives who came through from Germany and then Japan. It wasn't far from where she'd just let a phone call put her to her knees, for which she was ashamed. She quit being ashamed. Hands and knees and ashamed was nobody she knew.

The unit was back from a side street of low houses and built into a small barn that, years before, would have been some part of the business. It was still early spring and off-season, and none of the decent motels were open. She locked the car and went inside and smelled cigarettes. She took off her suit and shook loose a bit of sand. The shoes were fine.

She turned out the light and lay down on top of her bed, still feeling a punch deep into her stomach. She heard Remy saying, "You're out." She heard Ezekiel Parsons saying, "Are you okay?" She put those voices out of her mind. She had work to do.

⅄

The next morning, she woke sore and stiff. She cracked some windows to air out what she could of the old cigarette smoke. It was not quite light when she went out her door, but she could tell it would be a gray day. She wore a three-quarter wool coat that would survive rain. She wore pants and sturdy shoes. She walked down across the bottom of a main street, past low houses and an Italian deli, an Italian bakery. Elizabeth was the last place she would leave until she caught on as somebody else's funeral director for less money, if she did catch on. She put that thought away. She would do the job right, which was the only way she knew how—also the only way she could make Baxter guilty enough to give the can't-bear-to-lose-her recommendation she'd need. It wasn't too soon to start looking, but she didn't have the heart for it yet.

She walked fast, heading down to the harbor. Even in the half-dark, she could sense it between buildings. As she got near and the security lights timed off, she angled to the left past refrigeration units and transfer docks and dry storage, all of it beat up. She cut back toward the water through an alley of corrugated siding and came out on a wharf exactly where she'd thought she wanted to be.

Down to her right were the small boats tied to one another in pods. Directly across from her was the old plant. The last brand decoration was peeling off, but the dock and building looked solid.

All right, she'd seen this side of the plant, which she needed to do, but that wasn't what she'd really come for.

She'd come to thank Ezekiel Parsons, which was something you did. If somebody was kind, you thanked them. Also, Carol, for her own sake, had to face the fact that she'd been on her knees. That wasn't how she knew herself, and she would have preferred to forget it all, including this guy who had seen her, but Carol had never had the smarts-education-background-looks-connections that would let her forget inconvenient things. She got where she got by facing up to who she was and what that meant about how much harder she had to work and how much longer she had to keep going and how much less she had to hope for even when she was hoping for everything. She didn't have practice admitting heartbreak to a stranger, but common sense told her to come and stand in front of Ezekiel Parsons.

The relief was that Ezekiel Parsons's fishing boat was not where it ought to have been. Parsons was gone, and she had now seen the harbor side of the old plant. She could go. She'd made the effort and could send a thank-you card.

Because of her sentimental appreciation for old industry sites, she took a moment to register the irregular, decaying backs of the buildings that led to the plant. Weather and salt had worked at the paint on the buildings until the colors were a succession of grays and weathered pastels. She thought of her neighborhood as a kid, not something she thought of often, the pastels of those houses, though pastel on purpose. She could see the passageway that cut under and through the plant, the passageway she'd walked last night. Just beyond the plant was a tall, narrow icehouse where boats, as she understood it, picked up the ice for preserving their catch. It had the plant's wharfing and was functional and looked functional, but it was hardly new. Beyond that, water separated the end of the spit from the reach and run of the neck that protected the inner harbor from the outer harbor. The neck had a dry dock that looked like a factory skeleton, great rusted stanchions pointed up at angles around railroad tracks that ran into the water. Along beside that were more of the backs of the sort of harbor shops that ran to the plant, interspersed with two short piers of winter-shut restaurants. Looking straight out along the dock she stood on, Carol got glimpses of the outer harbor that opened largely away to a major breakwater and ocean. She couldn't see to the breakwater because of a fog gathering as the sun came up. In fact, the fog was rolling in heavily and fast, already darkening the early day. Time for Carol to get on with things. She turned and started back the way she'd come, to circle the head of the inner harbor and find her way around to the front of her plant.

"No, no," somebody said slow and singsong. "You don't get away that quick."

Without realizing it, she'd been looking across at her plant and around the inner harbor through a branch of communications junk and the tops of a couple of blunt hoists.

He said, "Easy is fine. It's what everybody calls me." He stood well below her on the deck of his boat, beside a great rusted industrial spool of rope nets. He wore boots and jeans and, cold though it was, just a white T-shirt. He was strong but way past a kid, the full head of hair starting to gray, legs too short and arms too big, a small hard pot for his belly. He stood with his legs apart. A working guy.

"I also really do have a harmonica," he said. "If you were wondering."

The deck of his boat looked like a factory floor. The booms came up in a "v" off the mast, and she might have touched the boom on her side, with its cable and its hanging iron plow. Down in the deck was a tangle of more cable, of winches and generators and more net and the gauges and the iron levers to drive it all.

"Since you asked," he said, "I grew up here, fishermen after fishermen, poor branch of a nice old name. But then I went to the Army, and it was one thing and another."

Carol didn't speak. She concentrated on her surroundings. This was the kind of factory floor she had been shutting down for years, and she would have liked to see it run. It was the kind of factory floor her father would have worked in early days, before OSHA and the rest. It was too crowded and with too much open gearing not to chew up arms and legs, and yet here it was, too efficient in its niche to die. Carol thought that was interesting.

Easy said, "I ended in the Mississippi Delta, married, fishing, shrimp to start, friends with good, simple people."

The day was coming as gray and cold as she'd expected. The boat was black and rust and pitted white, the loose net a damp, heavy tangle.

He was looking up at her, and she looked back at him instead of at his boat. She didn't have anything to say, and he seemed to get that. He was trying to help.

He said, "I once got a phone call like the one you got last night. It ended up sending me back home to this harbor."

His face was wide and his eyebrows almost touched. He had high cheekbones, and seamed wrinkles from working out of doors. He had a real chin with an old scar. It wasn't an ugly face, but it wasn't handsome either.

She could have shivered from being cold if she let herself. She said, "I would be afraid for the men on your floor, especially if there were waves."

He watched her, the kind of man she'd spent her life putting out of business, the kind of man she'd expected to wind up loving.

She said, "I'm sorry," and he nodded at her as if she knew him and as if her sympathy were important.

She also said, "I should have knocked."

He smiled at that, though she hadn't thought to be funny. He looked around for what she might knock on.

"Thank you for last night," she said. "You were very kind."

He said, "Come knock anytime," and she couldn't imagine a practical reason for that. As soon as she buried the fish company, she'd be gone back to New York to get herself a new job. She didn't believe she'd ever see Easy Parsons again, but she wished she would.

She waved good-bye, and she got going. She cut across through a dirt parking lot above the small boats and the guys getting ready to take those boats out. She wanted to take a look inside the old plant before she met Parks at the new plant.

As she reached the potholes on the lane out to the plant, she passed another lane that ran off at an angle through a warren of old clapboard duplexes. The first house on the corner had a sign saying, "St. Peter's Breakfast." She would have missed it if she hadn't smelled the bacon.

Thick fog was pouring in with daybreak, and she walked down the lane to the plant past a lobster outfit, and then there were the outbuildings for Elizabeth's Fish and the run of the plant itself behind its Cyclone fencing. She got out the keys Parks had given her. She felt the cold damp of the fog wrap onto the skin of her hands and face; the arms of her coat were shined with it. She wondered what it was like to work in her fisherman's factory when there was fog to go with the waves.

She stood in the spot where she'd talked to Remy on the phone last night, where she'd knelt. Ancient history.

The sun would be up soon, but the day was getting darker and colder. She walked along the fence, dragging one hand over the cold, slick crisscrossings until she reached the gate. She couldn't immediately find the right key to the padlock, but she got through and found the entry to the plant floor and unlocked those locks and stood facing a darkness of machinery. She was prepared to braille every wall to find light switches, but then decided that for the moment she didn't need to see.

Parks had told her the lines were still here. She would have expected the fat boys to have sold them. Carol wondered if the lines were connected to whatever faucet the fat boys still had their hands on. She stood in the doorway to the cavern of the plant. She could smell the shellac of old cooking. Beneath that, she could smell generations of fish dried to vapor. She could smell the life of this town that had gutted millions of pounds of the swimming life of the ocean. She could feel the scales of the fish on her like the fog, and she could sense the motion of the men who did the cutting in the days when a lot of that must have been handwork. The moment a bulldozer's blade first pierced a wall, all of that would begin to seep out, and then the building would get ripped to rubble and carted away.

Baxter had brought her on and sent her to one factory after another. She'd always understood that he saw her worth, and she'd also understood that as soon as he didn't think she was worth enough, he'd cut her loose. Blume, she'd thought, was the one who liked her. She imagined going back into the New York office. Would Blume have the balls to break the news? Baxter would promise to make the right calls for her, insist they plan a long lunch.

Outside in the fog she felt her way back along the fence and back to St. Peter's Breakfast. There she sat at the counter among half a dozen old men who continued to get up early even though the fish were gone and they themselves were done with trying to catch them, or sort and cut them. She ordered two bowls of oatmeal, a banana, strawberries, and nonfat cottage cheese, and when St. Peter told her none of that was available, she had two eggs up, bacon, and a short stack with extra syrup, and while she ate, the fog lifted enough for her to see her way back to this month's home and her car.

⅄

At the new plant, she found Parks and Annette, the financial second, in Parks's office.

Carol didn't say "Good morning." She said, "Take me onto the floor. Let's get it over with."

Parks told his assistant to call down. Everybody'd been prepped.

Carol led Parks and Annette along the hall with its glimmering fish wallpaper, and like a warden bringing no reprieve, she came out onto a mezzanine above the plant floor. It was a new factory, and it was big for Elizabeth Island, and you knew from the meticulous hum that it was state-of-the-art. But it was still not nearly a big enough plant to compete with the really big outfits that controlled the market now. The last twenty people who worked the floor were gathered beneath the mezzanine.

Once upon a time, Carol would have wanted to make the fat boys witness the announcement, but they wouldn't have cared.

Carol always made a point of looking at, and seeing, the people she was letting go. She looked now, and looked again. All twenty of the people on the floor were women.

She was surprised. She'd shut down women before, but not a lot, and she'd come ready for men. That shouldn't have made a difference, except that today it did. Carol was a woman, too, and she was being shut down herself.

Carol walked down the stairs and stood in the middle of the floor with her feet apart and her hands on her hips. She spoke louder than she needed.

She said, "I think you all know what the deal is. I've come here to shut this place down and shut it down for good. This equipment is going to go somewhere else. Maybe the building will be used for some purpose or other—it will be, if I do my job well—but Elizabeth's Fish is all done, and I'm sorry to tell you that. We'll work it out for you as best we can. What we owe you, we'll pay you. What we can get for you, we'll get for you. You've seen it coming. Today's the day, and I am sorry. Dave Parks is here, and his door is open. So is mine."

She stood silent. She looked around at the faces facing her. She met every eye that wanted her.

She realized she was waiting for Baxter to make his bodyguard call.

Then she realized he was not going to call her this last time, and that felt like its own surprise, on top of everything else. Carol, just like these women, was out of a job.

Instead of walking to the stairs and up off the floor, Carol said, "There is this." She did not say it as loudly or officially as she had been speaking. She said it like a conversation wandering.

Some of the women who had begun to turn away turned

back. As well as smocks, all of them wore surgical green bags over their hair, and Carol should have put one on before she came out.

She said, "I've just been down to the old plant."

She had never said anything like this before. She didn't know where she was going with it, but she was going.

And it came to her, this instant, Baxter's knee-jerk, how she and these women might be able to stand up. She wasn't anywhere near positive it would work, but she was not ready to let these women, or herself, go.

She said, "I understand that all the old lines are still in there, and that they still work."

She said, quietly enough that several of the women had to lean in to hear, "I'm going to see if that building and that equipment might support some reduced sort of operation. If it will, I'm going to get it running, and I'm going to need you people. It may not be a likely thing, and you may not want any part of it, but I'm going to figure it out fast and let you know fast. Think about it. Meanwhile, instead of pulling the plug right now, I'm going to ask you to keep doing your jobs here so that, no matter what happens, we can use up the inventory here and make a few extra bucks to divvy out."

The Second Half

Dave wondered why the hell Carol MacLean had just teased those women on the floor with the possibility of more work.

When he and Carol and Annette got back to his office, he shut the door, and Carol again gestured for him to sit at his desk. She even said "Please." It was a nice gesture, and since he had seen her commandeer Mathews's desk, Dave noted the gesture. Carol sat in one of the two snazzier-than-necessary chairs on the other side of the desk. Annette waited for Dave to signal that it was all right for her to sit in the other snazzy chair.

He nodded at her. Annette was not shy, but she was in her fifties now and had never spent much time off the island or, as they said, "over the bridge." She had black hair going gray in a bun; she wore baggy cardigans; she had a hopeful face. She was not imposing and wouldn't have wanted to be, and right now she was amazed almost to paralysis by Carol MacLean, the businesswoman from New York. When Carol asked Annette to remind her of her last name, it was all Annette could do to produce the "Novato."

To her further credit, Carol smiled at Annette in a friendly, unbig-shot way.

Then she turned to Dave. In his dreams, Dave had a great poker face, which he didn't, as his poker buddies would testify. Carol leaned her elbows on her knees, which were next to the HR magazines with their high-gloss covers advertising the thrill of workers' comp issues and making the most of the older worker.

"Dave, you think I was lying to the women on the floor about the hope of more work so I could keep them on task as long as possible and with as little loss as possible out the back door."

So much for the poker face. But Dave could still read people. He watched Carol.

She said, "There's background you don't know that prompted me to say what I did. If I find out we can make the old plant go, I'll tell you the background. But I wasn't kidding."

Fair enough. Carol looked like a capable businesswoman on her game, not somebody who'd tease those women on the floor to cut corners. But Dave wasn't ready to roll over just yet.

Annette had opened a notebook on her lap and was ready to hear her assignment so she could go back to her desk and do her best.

Carol turned to her and said, "Annette, you're in the room because Dave likes you. Because Dave likes you, I like you. Whether for a couple weeks or a lot longer, we three are going to be running the company. So please put your notebook down for a minute."

Annette closed her notebook and put her hands over it but couldn't let it off of her lap.

Dave decided to get it moving. He said, "The old plant works.

We've only been out of it a couple of months. What do you need to know?" He put some demand in his voice, and Carol didn't seem to mind.

She said, "I thought you'd been in here longer than that."

Which wasn't what he was asking, but okay, for the moment. "That was the pretense," he said. "We took the new address and touted the facility to the Germans and worked the old plant all the way out the fourth quarter because we got, or we booked, results that didn't yet reflect the cost-return equation of running the new plant at quarter capacity."

Dave didn't like hearing himself say those thoughts out loud, but she didn't look too surprised.

She said, "If the Japanese had waited much longer to buy, the Germans would have had to see what was going on." Which was the truth, and Dave knew it.

He said, "Maybe the Germans didn't want to know, or the Japanese. So, yeah, Mathews was lucky, but he also worked at it. By the time you guys bought in, I imagine he had about worked every angle."

In fact, Dave suspected that Mathews might have had a whole separate filing system of records and projections that could be worked in the dark as the company wound down.

It seemed Carol had suspicions of her own. "Annette," she said, "I sense there's another angle working. Do you have any idea what else Mathews and the others are selling? How they're going to get their last nickel?"

Dave interrupted before Annette could answer. "Good question, Carol," he said. "But let's get straight who's asking and why. We thought we were just going to help put this company out of its misery. If something else, like a new company, is happening, let's be clear about it. The old plant is funky, but we've got people who can turn the lights on. They can turn the key for the whole operation. That plant works. So, if you're really not jerking us around, I think you ought to tell us about this secret background of yours."

Carol looked glad for the chance to unload, and Dave sat back, lie detector switched on.

She said, "After this burial, I was supposed to get a promotion from Baxter Blume. Last night, I found out the promotion is going to someone else, and once I'm done here, I'm out at Baxter Blume. I was going to continue burying Elizabeth's Fish as if nothing had happened, do a good job, and get Baxter Blume to say good things about me. Then I went on the floor and saw the women. I've seen plenty of women in plants, but I didn't expect them here, and I realized I wasn't any different from them. I was another woman on the way out. When I realized that, I didn't want to just lie down and get shoved out any more than I wanted to shove those other women. I said what I said off the top of my head, but I've got good business instincts, and there are ingredients in the circumstances here. I'm not smart enough to play everything Mathews and the other fat boys were playing, but I trust my instincts. I was supposed to be promoted. Instead of burying companies, I was supposed to get a company of my own. I still want that. I want to spend my time keeping a company alive. We might, you and I and Annette, have a shot with that old plant."

Well. No shit. She was talking past the edges of sound business, but she was also talking about serious personal risk for herself. Even if she got fired, when she got back to New York, she'd still be around the business at that level in the big leagues. If she stayed here, it wouldn't take long for her to be out of the loop for good. She knew that, and she was signing on regardless, which

counted big-time as far as Dave was concerned. She was also asking Dave and Annette to take a risk, but they didn't have nearly as
much to lose as she did.

No question she'd need him if she was going to buy the plant.
She probably didn't know yet that she'd also need Annette, but
that would become apparent.

Dave stood up behind his desk. He turned on his radio, and
a familiar dree-ee-ee-eam came out low. He snapped his fingers
once and did a very quick guitar move—not to frighten the new
leader of the pack.

Some people, handling a situation, sweated through their
clothes. Not Dave. He joined the band in this kind of deal. He
didn't have a clue about Carol MacLean. Or Annette. He spun
around to take in his windowsill. Pictures of grown daughters.
Picture of the last steel mill, into which you could fit fifty of this
new fish plant. Bent putter and a bad-luck golf glove. Golf hat
from Augusta that his wife got him when he couldn't go. Child-
size football helmet on a plaque beside the pictures of the kid
teams he coached. Then on that wall beside the window, a big
watercolor painting of the old and then-still-active Elizabeth's
Fish plant from across the harbor. Good picture. A plant he
liked more than he'd admitted to Carol when they were down
there.

Dave got back to the radio and shucked his blazer off. He
wore a green necktie and a white dress shirt with Ralph Lau-
ren's little polo player. If somebody like Carol's boss Baxter saw
the polo player, he'd know that Dave was deep in the minor
leagues.

He rolled up his sleeves and sat back down as if his desk were
a jacked Fairlane, and he asked Annette, serious question, "Yes?"

Carol, looking confused, said, "Maybe this stays among us for a while. What I said on the floor will go around town, but let's not chat about it with Baxter Blume. I'm not going to cheat Baxter Blume, but I'm thinking we could do right by everybody, and if Baxter Blume finds out too soon, they might decide to get me off the property as fast as I got the fat boys off."

Dave turned down the radio to get this. He had just pretty much decided to trust Carol. So he hated to hear her say they weren't going to cheat her old boss, especially after she'd just gotten done saying she hadn't lied to the women on the floor. Nixon came to mind: Your president is not a liar and a cheater.

Carol said, "Nothing changes with this new plant." She looked at Dave as if she could read his mind. "It's a high-volume, low-margin plant with way too much debt to overcome. Even if we could afford to buy it from Baxter Blume and take it through bankruptcy, we'd have a long haul rebuilding and expanding the brand. And we'd probably never get to capacity competing with similar but much larger operations working at less than capacity for established brands fifty miles south and a hundred miles north. You know all that. So on behalf of Baxter Blume, we sell everything we can for the best we can get, and Elizabeth's Fish goes into the ground, and whatever debt we don't put into the ground at the same time, that goes to work for Baxter Blume. I came here to make this happen, and I want it done right. Only, while we're selling everything else, we also sell the old plant, debt free but at established fair value, to ourselves, to a new company that we're going to run. When we get to that part of the process, we talk to Baxter Blume. If we get the name cheap, maybe we take the name. Maybe not. But if we aren't squeaky clean going to Baxter Blume, they'll know and they'll hit us over the head."

They couldn't yet know how the numbers would play out,

but what Carol said, and how she said it, made sense to Dave. He had been in business long enough to see bodies, so he knew when to leave the room. At least he hoped he did. For now, he was staying in.

Carol said, only to Annette, "We'll figure out, mostly you'll figure out, whether the old plant, free of debt, will buy itself and provide enough money for us to get traction. Will it still have some market? Do we need employee stockholders to pay the bills until we have traction?"

Dave nodded at Annette to go for it.

She said to Carol, "You're asking whether it's even possible that we ever actually would get traction."

Carol said, "That's the sixty-four-thousand-dollar question," and Dave watched it happen as Annette stepped up as a player for the first time.

Carol, on the other hand, looked nervous for the first time. Dave wondered if she was having second thoughts about throwing what was left of her career out the window. Please, God, he thought, don't let her be worrying about whether she'd be stupid enough to put her own money at risk. That kind of thing could be contagious, and Dave didn't want to be around it. What would her guy Baxter have to say about that kind of risk?

Baxter Blume had taken this company on so cheaply that there hadn't been real need to run, or time to run, even a feint at due diligence. Which was why Dave believed Carol didn't know shit about this company. Carol was risking enough by going forward on a hunch and with people she'd just met. There was no way she would invest her own money, Dave thought.

Carol was focused on Annette. She had asked Annette whether there could be traction, and Annette was thinking.

Annette said, "Yes."

She said it to Carol, and then turned and said it to Dave. "Yes."

Annette put her notebook down on the floor and leaned forward and said it again. "Yes."

Carol looked at Dave to see if he was letting Annette call it.

Annette said, "It will have traction."

Dave nodded back to Carol and said, "Absolutely."

Outside, rain had begun to hit the window hard, but inside was stillness, and Dave watched Carol considering. At some point she'd have to consider whether the women she'd talked to on the plant floor would and could deliver.

She looked at Dave and said, "The women are solid, right?"

The women were different generations of Elizabeth Island Yankees and Italians and Portuguese, some with faces like Annette's, some paler, some darker, some harder. There were also Asian and South American workers now. Dave knew them to be, all of them, good workers, and he believed they would jump at the chance of starting up again in the old plant.

He said, "No question."

Carol grinned at him and back at Annette.

Dave said, "So, what about the three of us?"

And Carol said, "I am in. I am going after this new company, period. I'd sure like to hear the two of you say that you're in."

"Commitment's good, especially when getting close to a corpse. Well, I like the corpse. I'm in, Carol, and I'm glad to be in with you, and glad to be with Annette, if she's in."

Annette said, "In," very loud, and then laughed at how loud, and both of them laughed with her, and then Carol said, "Okay. Let's get started." And the laughter stopped.

Carol was a natural leader, which was something you felt, and Dave felt it, and it looked as if Annette did, too.

FREDERICK DILLEN

Carol said, "Annette, I'd like you to start working up valuations for everything we're going to unload, in individual pieces and in various likely packages. While you're doing that, please keep an eye out for however the fat boys are still ripping off the company. I know I mentioned it before, but I'd be amazed if they didn't have something going."

"Fat boys? The other senior executives, you mean?"

"Yes, forgive me."

"No. They are fat."

Dave didn't have to be reminded why he liked Annette, but he liked being reminded.

Annette said, "There is that electricity that began disappearing at the old plant almost a month ago."

Carol looked to Dave, who spread his hands. He'd mentioned it to her in passing because Annette had mentioned it to him.

Annette said, "I talked to the utilities. They've checked their readings, and that's all they can tell me. I figure we can't afford to send electricians in to follow all the wiring. I did have somebody check the smoke alarms, though, and I told the Fire Department to be ready to come fast, in case. But I don't think it is the wiring."

Now, Dave suspected, Carol might be getting it about Annette. Decent person, hard worker, capable, self-starting, loyal, fresh perspective, not allergic to details. There were only so many Annettes in the world, and they had one.

"All right," Carol said. "Thank you. Keep the electricity in mind, and keep looking everywhere else. Dave, I need you to be thinking big picture in terms of industry demand for what components we have and where that demand is and also what we may need for ourselves. And right, we need figures, as complete as we can get, for the old plant. If you guys can help one another, great.

You decide which of the office staff we should keep on. We may want to keep everybody, or not. If I can help you in anything, tell me. The disposal stuff I'm good at. Some of it I'll handle entirely, but I'm also at your mercy on the details. Getting up the new company, we already have a template at the old plant, but we'll need to rethink that as well. No question, we'll have to find ways to boost the margins, and I think we'll be looking for specialty niches. You guys, please, say anything. This is a team, and I've got skills, but I don't know much about your business in general or this company in particular."

Annette said, "But Baxter Blume has everything about us, don't they?"

Dave shook his head.

Annette said, "No?"

Carol said, "They bought very quickly and even more cheaply, and due diligence all but went out the window. I mean, I know a little bit about the industry and its trajectory, a little bit about a shop like yours using blocks of shredded and frozen fish from Asia to feed your lines. Aside from that, no. As far as the detailed news inside this company, no. I hope you won't think of me as a dope."

"On that note," Dave said, and he was happy to see Carol laugh. Annette laughed, too, when she was sure it was okay.

"Actually," Dave said, "there are a couple of things you might want to do today, or today and tonight, while Annette and I dig for evidence, criminal and otherwise, around here. First, there's a conference going on today in the high school gymnasium. Fishermen from up and down the coast, government officials, oceanographic experts, environmental types, industry representatives, some civic reps. There's a common understanding that the fish stocks in the Atlantic are mostly gone, and that the fishing industry is responsible. Knowledgeable fishermen on the harbor here contend that the stocks are coming back, but this conference is probably going to confirm a draconian amendment to fishing regulations about how much fish and what kind can be taken when and where. The amendment would put a lot of fishermen out of business, the ones that aren't out already. Not a good thing for our new enterprise, but not necessarily the end of the world. It could be the amendment won't happen, but in any case, you're right—the fish we need for our fish sticks is coming in frozen blocks mostly from Asia. I'm thinking you might want to look in on all this. You'd get a flash cross section of the business and what's happening in it."

"And the second thing? Tonight?"

"Every four years, the town council meets, in front of a lot of the town, to decide whether or not to keep the waterfront zoned for the fishing industry only. That zoning is a matter of town pride, but the harbor is dying. At every one of these meetings, going back awhile, there's been more and more agitation to break the zoning restriction and cash in on commercial development of the waterfront property. It's rare that these would happen on the same day, but the zoning meeting is set in stone, and the thing at the gym is short notice and urgent. Consider yourself lucky, Carol."

She grinned. "I'm there for both events."

And while Carol was at the high school, Dave was going to look for Mathews's secret files.

Dave could hardly believe the old plant was waking from the dead. He stood back up and said in his sports announcer voice, "Yes. The team is coming out to play the second half."

High School for Fishermen

Carol walked over to the high school from her apartment. She walked fast. She was eager. No more waiting for somebody to hand over a company. Carol was in motion, on her own, grabbing a company of her own.

The high school was fifties modern, and around the edges of the parking lot were the fishermen's pickups and flatbeds, most of them hard-used. The rest of the parking lot was kids' cars. Carol had never been back to her own high school, but over the years she'd gone to other high schools for meetings with workers and townspeople as factories were shut. No matter how tough the times, the kids had cars.

For Carol, cars had meant the alley she knew as a kid. She'd made her friends there. They were older, though less older as new kids came in and the bigger kids left for real jobs or the draft. By the time Dominic came, Carol had her job getting parts for the alley. She used that money to buy her own parts for the bent-frame, free-if-you-haul-it-away Mustang that her dad paid the towing for. Dominic was taller than she was, which few of them were because she got her height early and a lot of it. He was also only three years older, though that could seem plenty in those days. What was important was that Dominic knew about car engines and how to work on them. And because she didn't realize how good he was at first, she did a crazy thing. She took his hand and said she'd introduce him to the parts guys at the store. He laughed and made her pull him all the way, leaning back but not letting go of her hand. When they reached the store, she told the guys to please help him out since he might want to get parts on his own.

Carol kept her hands in her pockets all the way back to the alley. Then Dominic grabbed her hand out of her pocket when she'd relaxed. He pulled her to where his hood was leaning on a boarded door down the alley. She hadn't seen that he'd cut it and had a scoop ready. She couldn't believe she hadn't noticed. She had suggested a standard barrel because he didn't look cool enough. Then she looked at the cut for the scoop, and it was very clean, and when she looked at him, he shrugged.

Except he was still holding her hand, which he also thought was funny, and she did, too, after half-pretending to be mad. So he was like a brother at first, and she didn't have a brother. Then they were best friends, and later everything else besides.

High school for her as a kid, if anybody there had noticed, was the wrong clothes with the wrong face and the wrong body. She didn't care. Her life was in the alley.

When she was at high school gyms for meetings to bury factories, she was invisible to the kids just by virtue of being an adult. Around Baxter Blume, she was mostly invisible because she was gone so much, besides which, she was a colleague nobody had to compete with, doing a job nobody else wanted. Long before Remy's call, she'd become a parochial throwback who was never going to get near the front of the line. Susannah wouldn't know where to find a suit like the ones Carol wore. Susannah was going to participate in the equity funds sooner or later regardless of having to babysit the company Carol had wanted. Had Susannah ever had to compete with Carol? What had there been to compete with? The Beast? She had been sent to six weeks of a summer sales management course at not-really Harvard, of which she was very proud at the time but which she knew would be a joke to people with real colleges. Now she was out at Baxter Blume, and out as an undertaker, and those were good things. As she walked through today's parking lot toward the gym doors, the Beast was nowhere near.

Carol was not coming to the town gym to bury anybody; she was coming to get a reading on her industry.

She was not coming here to see Easy Parsons, but as soon as Parks had mentioned the meeting, she had understood she might.

The signage sent her in a side door and down a hall of trophy cases. The listed participants in the meeting were acronyms: state and federal ocean regulatory and research agencies, environmental interest groups, fishermen's civic and industry groups. She could hear a cheap sound system working against a basketball court's height of girders and banners. This was like no meeting she would ever have held; there would be discussion here, it seemed. When Carol had showed up to run a meeting, there had been no discussion. Still, she'd had to face gymnasiums full of people hoping she'd change her mind, as if she'd had a mind to change. She'd listened and answered to be respectful, but her answers were never long. This meeting had nothing directly to do with her, and she was glad it didn't. Despite whatever discussions, it was essentially a bad-news meeting, and instinctively her stomach fisted tight. Since she had no intimate investment in the bad news, she felt as if she were stopping to look at these people's blood in a wreck beside the road. Although they had some hope of a good outcome, Parks had said. Would they all really be here if there was no hope? She didn't know.

She stepped through the double doors to a wall of the backs of workingmen who stood in flannel shirts and fiberfill vests, men she had put out of work by the thousands, men with whom her father had belonged and with whom she should have belonged.

For a shamefully long time, Carol didn't think of her father when she was shutting down plants and factories. But once she did, she imagined him every time among the men she faced—and despite the women at Elizabeth's Fish this morning, it was usually mostly men. She had looked at the faces she fired to give them what humanity she could. She had come to look doubly hard because she never knew which face was going to turn out to be her father, and she wanted him to know she loved him and was sorry and didn't expect his forgiveness and hoped to have it anyhow. That was a lot to put in a look, ridiculous if you thought about it, certainly nothing you talked about. Just the same, it was real, and it was hard work to stand straight and tough enough to keep anyone from imagining the weakness of second thoughts. Her father wouldn't have wanted to see weakness either. His proudest moment would have been hearing about her six weeks studying new sales management techniques in a summer classroom on the Harvard campus. He had died the year before, but when she was on the campus, she had told him, out loud, where she was, and she had imagined he could hear.

She edged through the men as if she didn't notice she was taller than many of them. When she was inside, she could see that the bleachers were crowded with more men, and still more men sat in the folding chairs set out across the floor. Two hundred fishermen? Three hundred? These men, just like the men she'd had to face year after year, whatever their trade, looked achingly out of place. They'd been boys in gyms like this and they weren't boys now. Beyond the rows of chairs was the U of tables for the managers and scientists and advocates and whoever was the senior bringer of bad news.

She took a flyer off a bleacher bench. Apparently conservationists had offered an amendment to radically tighten federal legislation that governed the days and territories and catch weights for boats that went out after groundfish in New England's Atlantic fishing areas. Groundfish were the heart of the industry. A judge supported the amendment, and if the agencies decided to enforce it as scheduled in a few weeks, most of the men here wouldn't fish again. That did not sound good for them, and Carol sympathized, but for her own company, she wasn't sure what it meant. Parks had told her that the blocks of fish to feed the lines in the old plant would in fact come from Asia, and presumably that supply wouldn't be affected by what happened here.

Today the agencies were announcing their decision, and if it had been her, Carol would have convened the meeting and made the announcement fast and let the fishermen get to the bars.

Wherever they were from—Maine, Gloucester, New Bedford, Rhode Island, Connecticut, Long Island—the fishermen were old. The men who were standing were healthy, but even they were forty years old. The guys sitting in the chairs, from behind she could see their rolls and their bald spots and their white bristle on loose jowls. Carol wondered if all these fishermen would really have come from such distances if this was the kind of no-hope show she used to run. Parks had said, after all, that the amendment and the regulations might not get approved.

Maybe, Carol thought, Elizabeth Island had been lucky in losing most of its fleet earlier than the harbors with bigger fleets and auction sites. She had seen it before. As industries consolidated and transformed and were killed off, the towns and companies that hung on longest sometimes got hit hardest in the end, while ravaged companies in the towns that got hit first had time to discover niches and adapt and survive.

As soon as she thought that, Carol wondered what might be a profitable niche her company could establish.

For her plant here to survive, it would need to find and fill some sort of niche to augment the failing margins in its principal product of fish sticks cut from those blocks of frozen fish brought in from overseas. Unless Carol could lower the price on her fish sticks, she could not compete with the bigger outfits in the business. Income from some sort of niche, and it didn't have to be a lot of income, would give her the leeway to lower her fish stick price.

What the plant didn't use, what it had been built for and survived on generation after generation, was fresh fish. It was the failing of fresh fish stocks that had led to importing blocks of frozen fish from Asia and that right now was killing the fishermen in this gym. Carol thought it might be possible that fresh fish, maybe even regardless of the regulations, could provide her plant with the balance of free cash flow that would mean survival. She wondered if there would be enough fresh fish available to give her a small signature niche, and to tip her balance sheet into the black.

She looked at the fishermen. She'd seen the factory floor of a fishing boat this morning, and she felt she could pick out the factory owners in the room by the authority in their bearing. She thought she spotted a brittle pretense in the posture of some of them, suggesting that their boats might belong to the bank in a month. It was the kind of dynamic you could notice among men anywhere.

There was a different dynamic in this gym, though, than there would have been in a gym full of other kinds of factory workers, and it wasn't just because there were a lot of independent owners here. There weren't any women. Ah, Carol thought, women worked in the plants, and men went out on the boats. But that didn't account for the discomfort she felt in her head and her stomach. She felt unsteady on her feet.

Had she eaten something? Suddenly she could barely stand. Blume thought she was too old a zebra.

She looked over the heads of the men in the chairs to the table of short-sleeve-dress-shirted, cheap-necktied deputy commissioners and assistants to directors and low-level scientists and the few wrinkled guys who were just fishermen representing fishermen. She was too unsteady to tell who was speaking, but somebody's voice came through the gym with the dooming command of all bureaucrats pretending to move things along.

She looked away from that and up at the far wall to calm her stomach. A great wooden plaque told which school basketball players had scored the most points ever. The best, with more than two thousand points, had graduated in 1962. But the second best, also with more than two thousand, had graduated only the year before. Elizabeth Island must have had a team. Carol was glad for them. As an awkward kid who spent most of her time in her alley with older guys and her bent Mustang, she'd never gone to her high school's games. But as an undertaker, when she was in a town for the only reason she was ever in a town, she always hoped that some team was winning.

A new voice came, and it was familiar. It was Easy, just like Carol had hoped. She could tell he was at home with himself and that he had real news whether or not his peer fishermen had enough political or economic weight to warrant him saying it. Carol was more interested just in looking at him. He wore old khakis and a flannel shirt over a long-sleeve undershirt, and the sleeves of both shirts were rolled up to his elbows. She looked at the hair on his strong forearms and wondered, like a teenager, if he was handsome.

She quieted everything in her stomach and listened to his slow, assured persuasion. You knew he was one of the guys who made a living, and he seemed to think he could keep doing it. He explained that his vessel was rigged so he could go to species or location the minute they opened. Other people could do the same. Derby fishing, he called it. Carol had come thinking the fishermen couldn't make it work, and it turned out she was wrong, which was interesting. And yet, what was strangest to Carol was that as she watched Easy, she felt an alarm deep inside herself. She hadn't felt that—though there had been other men—since she was a teenager with Dominic.

She looked away to the men standing just to the right and behind her, and they were standing the same way Easy was standing. That was why she was losing her balance: they all stood as if the gym were rocking, as if the gym were a boat on water, and she was on it with them.

Carol was seasick, and as seasick as she felt, or because she felt so seasick, she was full of wonder that these men made their lives on the empty ocean, out of sight of land. She leaned toward the bleachers so she could hold on to the end of a bench.

To keep the seasickness away, she closed her eyes and imagined herself nowhere near the ocean. She thought about the alley and Dominic. He had a great car. He let her work on it with him, and he helped with the beat-up Mustang she'd bought, but only when she needed muscle or extra hands—she didn't ever want to think she was not the one who did what she did. His dad was dead. He only had his mother like Carol only had her father. You were a different person if one of your parents was dead, and Carol thought it made Dominic kinder, not that he didn't kick ass in his car. Then they found out it was a law that if you were the only son of a widow, you didn't get drafted, although that hardly mattered at first. What mattered was, to begin with, they got to be friends so fast. It was as one-two-three as sunup, no question. But friends were one thing. The other guys in the alley were friends, even if never like her with Dominic. The crazy-as-science-fiction part was that she knew ahead of time that he loved her, when anybody else would have thought it was still only cool-Dominic and just-Carol, car pals. She never planned, or even honestly understood, what she hoped. Simply one day she knew past all that, which shouldn't seem brave but was as brave as she'd ever been. Since he didn't know yet. If she had told anybody, they would have laughed, but she knew, and she waited until he knew, too. He never acted like he was surprised, which for her was as kind as anything possible. He was going to have to kiss her. She could have said so, because that was obvious as having to have a Hurst shifter. All she did was smile, and he made like do-I-have-to, and pretty quick he did.

She opened her eyes, and she was in the fishermen's gym, and

Dominic was not here. Easy Parsons was walking past her, going out through the gym doors without having seen her.

She shoved herself away from the bleachers and followed him. In the hall, he was walking fast but not nearly as fast as Carol was thinking, and what she was thinking about, now that she had her focus back, was what she had to get right. In ten yards, she figured out her company's niche and how it had to work.

She caught up to him and said, "Please remember me, Mr. Parsons. Easy. I'm Carol MacLean, and I'm here to shut down the plant. Did I say that this morning?"

He nodded and smiled and said slow, teasing, "Won't you give me a hello?" She worried she had been too formal. That was a default posture. But the point was, she'd seen him on his boat, in his factory, this morning. Then, just now, she'd heard him capable and confident at the microphone. She'd sensed respect for him in the gym.

She got straight to the point. She said, "If I bought the old plant, could you and other boats in the harbor bring enough fresh fish to my dock so I could run a small but reliable sideline? With the big outfits bringing in frozen fish in blocks from Asia, I suspect the fishermen in the gym here are selling their catch to retail outlets through auctions or wholesalers, or both. I think I could find profit margins for the old plant and for some fishermen, if we bypassed the auctions and wholesalers, and their commissions, and I took fish directly off the boats and marketed it fresh and direct to close regional retail. We'd have to work the numbers, but I think they might be good."

Easy stopped beside the trophy case closest to the parking lot door and studied her and said, "Cash?"

He was a good-looking man with authority, and she couldn't help wanting to stand near him.

"Cash," she said.

"You know anything about fish?" he said and looked her up and down. Carol told herself to focus.

"No."

"But you know factories."

"I do."

"And you got a fish factory team."

"I think so."

"You want me on that team."

"Yes. I think I might."

"No, I'm telling you. You want me on that team. Why do I get the feeling you're making this up right this minute?" He was interested, and she wanted to answer him in a way that kept hold of him. She liked talking business with him in this hall.

She said, "Sometimes it happens that way."

He grinned, and his grin was all teasing, no business. He was not tall, but he was a big man just the same, and he said, slow enough that the beginning and the end barely touched, "Sweetheart, where've you been hiding?"

Carol liked when Easy teased her, but now she wasn't sure what it meant or if it was kind. She was no beauty; she knew that. So she ignored it and stayed on topic. "On the basketball court just now, I thought you were telling everybody that you could catch fish despite the regulations."

He said, "My groundfish stocks, my cod and haddock and most of the rest, are stabilized. That's what's really happening in there. The scientists say the stocks are level; the regulators say they're going to tell the judge to drop the amendment, and the conservationists say they won't argue."

That sounded good, but he sounded irritable.

She said, "I didn't know that. I thought they were going to keep the amendment and the regulations. I was relieved to think you'd still be able to catch fish."

He stood with his legs apart and his arms out from his sides and waited, definitely irritable, for her to explain why she hadn't known what the hell was going on before she talked business to him.

She let him wait. To make a real living at physical work now, you had to be seriously on the ball, and she admired his kind of guy, but he wasn't the first one she'd ever met.

He made an expression implying he was above the silent game. "When I said I could catch fish no matter what, it was only to tell the bureaucrats that a good decision was not a handout. If the amendment actually happened and the regulations went into effect, we'd all either die or take our boats to ports a thousand miles away. If you don't know any of this, Carol MacLean, why would you come to town one day and talk about buying an old fish plant the next?"

"Good question," she said. "We've got some thinking to do. But it could happen. If it does, I'll come find you."

She'd heard what she needed to hear, and she thought she'd be able to find him if she needed to.

Now, if they'd been in the parking lot, he could have headed for his truck, and since she was walking, she could have headed in any other direction, but they were still locked together in the hall, so he threw her a bone. "As it is under the old regs and with what we're catching these days, which isn't much, Elizabeth Island boats could bring a nice little business worth of fresh fish to your door. You're right—we'd save on fuel and time and probably auction cost, and you'd get a best price. Everybody makes out." Which he said sensibly and agreeably. He was a guy she could work with, so it had been a useful dawn visit that she'd made to his boat, and a useful visit here to the high school.

He opened the door to the raw damp of the parking lot, and Carol said, "Wonderful. Thank you," and focused on reading which way he was headed.

He headed nowhere.

He stood and held the door for her. Carol was not one of the women who objected to doors being held, but she was caught off guard, and he waited. He was teasing her, because she'd waited him out a moment ago with her silence. He looked ready to wait with his door for a month.

She brushed his arm as she walked through the door.

He smiled. He got serious again and said, "You know what else? And it ain't a small thing. If we keep that plant going, we keep the port going. It's always been a fishing port, and it should stay one. If we lose the plant, and the harbor zoning on its land, zoning on the whole harbor could become a free-for-all. The fish plant and everything else could go to condos in a heartbeat. That counts, Carol. We can do some good. Harbor zoning. I'm supposed to take my boat out, but I'll stick around another day to see what you come up with. I'll talk to other captains."

She reached and got his hand and shook it and said, "Thank you, Ezekiel."

He had a strong grip. She was glad she had a strong grip herself, but then she was nervous with them holding one another's hands, and she let go. He didn't let go. He looked at her with the kindness she'd almost forgotten, and he said, "I've heard what some people call you, and I don't approve of it. If I ever call you anything besides Carol, I'm going to call you Beauty."

She took a breath. He sounded like he meant well, but Carol's business from now on was her new company, and as soon as her company was going, the name would be history. She said, "Thanks, but I'm used to the name."

Another fisherman called out from across the parking lot, and Easy nodded to say good-bye to Carol and jogged off. Carol stayed where she was to let him get away. She watched him longer than she needed to.

When everybody in a town knew that you were Death, people sometimes pretended to be friends because they thought you could do things for them. She was more comfortable without those friends, though she made a point of always being courteous. Easy Parsons was something else. If she'd been asked what, aside from his fish, she most liked about him, she would have said it was that he didn't notice he was four inches shorter than she was. The Beauty part she could do without.

Time to move on, for the fat boys. Carol was convinced that they were working something to rip off the new plant. But now she wondered if they might have something going with the old plant. It had already been a long day, and she had some thinking to do.

She also had Dave Parks's second meeting tonight. She had time to get back to her apartment and close her eyes for a minute.

Instead of starting back, she watched Easy Parsons standing in a puddle and talking to the fisherman who'd called out to him. They stood together beside their trucks. All those boots in a puddle. They would be talking about her, she guessed. She wished she knew what they were saying.

Yes.

She ran across the parking lot between kids' cars and around puddles. Carol could run if she had to.

The meeting tonight in Town Hall was all about harbor zoning. If Mathews and the other fat boys bought the old plant, they could sell the equipment inside, equipment that still worked, for a fair dollar in South America or the Caribbean. But the big score, if the harbor zoning got lost, would be tearing down the plant and developing the site for a hotel or condos. If the fat boys could buy the site for what it was worth when zoned for harbor use only, they could buy cheap. Then, if they had been playing for this all along, and if the harbor zoning was abandoned tonight . . .

She called, "Easy," and he and the other fisherman watched her run to them like it was something they'd want to remember. Who cared? She cared, but not enough to slow down.

She guessed Easy would have told his friend that Carol wanted fish for the old plant. If keeping the harbor for fishing was serious to them, she had serious news. She got to their puddle and stood in it with them. She was not wearing oiled boots like they were. Cold water, price of admission.

Easy said to her, "Beauty."

What was that supposed to mean? With Beast, it had been forever since she'd had to think about keeping her mouth shut, but she had to think about it now. She had thought she was all business, and now she wasn't sure.

Easy kept on talking as if he knew her from some other neighborhood that had called her Beauty forever. He said, "This is Buddy Taormina. When Buddy goes out, I follow him to where the fish are. He runs two boats. You want to know Buddy. And Buddy, this is the Carol MacLean we've been hearing about, come to shut down Mathews and what's left of the company. Even when she's not standing in water without her boots on, I call her Beauty."

Oh come on, except he had a nice smile. He was teasing her, and he looked like he also thought she was a beauty. Carol was not used to that, but she was going to accept it. Why not? If he meant it, he meant it, and she said, "Another case of women, even beauties, having tougher feet than fishermen." He laughed, and so did his friend, but if he didn't mean it about her being a beauty, Easy Parsons had damn well better be a terrific fisherman.

She held out her hand to the friend, Buddy.

Buddy shook her hand and looked at Easy. Buddy had heard about the Beast. Everybody always had.

Easy said, "I also call her Beauty when she's not around. From now on, I figure we can all call her that when she's not around." He sounded like he'd been sent to get rid of the Beast and start things over all by himself, and like he was ready to go after anybody who didn't fall into line. Carol blushed. They were only words he was saying, but she felt them as if his callused hands were on her skin.

Buddy Taormina was taller than Easy but not as tall as she was. He was wide, and a bigger hand wrapped around her own big hand when they shook. He looked at Carol like she was a foreigner, which she was, and like he was a tough guy, which he was, and like he was content to call her anything.

She said, "Carol is fine," but it came out more faintly than usual.

Buddy said, "If you open up the old plant and start working fresh again, Easy and I will be happy captains, and we'll find you some other happy captains. We'll bring you good fish at a good price."

She nodded. She didn't look at Easy. She was a businesswoman. She was forty years past sixteen, and she wondered if she'd become one of the girls who giggled with boys in the parking lot. She'd never been one of those girls, and never wanted to be. After the alley, and after Dominic, she had worked because that was what she had and what she wanted, and that had become a long time. There had been men but not many and never for long, so being alone and wanting to be touched mattered less and less.

She said to Buddy, "Something tells me Mathews and his gang are going to try and buy the old plant."

She could see that rang bells with Buddy.

She said, "It's the zoning, isn't it?"

Out of the corner of her eye, she saw Easy straighten up. He said, "Fuck me."

Carol was glad for the voice. It brought her back.

Buddy said to Easy, "What's the matter with you?"

Easy said, "Sorry. But really. No, I never gave that a thought." Carol didn't mind the language a bit, and she nodded at Easy to let him know. Then Buddy said to her, "It's harbor industrial. Ordinarily, if they didn't do fish in there, they'd have to service boats some way."

"Ordinarily," Easy said in an ordinary voice that Carol heard in her own ordinary way. Business.

She said, in a businesslike voice, "I heard it from Parks, but I didn't put it together until just now."

Easy said, "Now it's so sacred that the town council only votes to open it up once every four years."

Yes, Carol thought. "And tonight's the night," she said.

"Beauty," Easy said quietly to himself like he was appreciating her business smarts. She appreciated them herself.

She was holding her coat over her arm, and she reached into a pocket for her cell phone.

Easy went over it out loud. "Finally everybody's ready to say the hell with fish zoning. Harbor property would be worth something, and condominiums will pay better taxes than the piers do anymore. The commuters have wanted to kill the harbor for years, museum it, pretend it makes them part of something without having to smell it."

"Marblehead it," Buddy said. "Berth their yawls."

"But the old plant is a big site," Easy said. "Mathews and the boys could fit a real hotel there."

Carol punched in Dave Parks on her cell. When he picked up, she said, "Dave, it's me. I'll bet Mathews is buying the old plant."

"We know," Parks said. "We just found the separate filing system in his office. He had had Annette do a cursory prospectus to sell the old plant, and then, without Annette or me suspecting a thing, and I would ordinarily have had to sign off, Mathews arranged a sale. He ran it outside the company, through a group of firms in Rhode Island. All the paperwork, all in order, fire-walled from operations in the rest of the company. The prospectus wouldn't satisfy a serious buyer, but they got a buyer."

"It's done? Dave. Don't tell me it's done."

"They made the sale as soon as we moved out of the old plant, with an appearance of selling the equipment along with the property for a genuine fish business, to satisfy the harbor-industrial zoning. There's a due diligence feint and a throwaway escrow, and because the property's zoned for fish business only, they bought at a great price."

Carol said, "Oh. God damn."

Parks said, "But here's the thing. It's a straw buyer. We're committed to the sale, but they don't have to make final commitment until next month, and they can pull out up until then. Well, do you remember me telling you about the meeting tonight, at the town hall? That the town only addresses zoning on the harbor every four years, to preserve the infrastructure and the character of the harbor and keep the Marbleheaders out? Well—"

"Tonight's the night," Carol said. Last night, she was finally getting a company of her own before she lost it, and then she actually got one this morning and lost it less than a minute ago, and just now, as the rain began again, she got it back. She shook out her coat and pulled the shoulders around herself and bent over to keep the phone dry.

Easy and Buddy, one of them on each side of her, lifted her coat so it covered her like a tent.

She was in the middle of the scariest business deal she'd ever been near, and she was giddy for two fishermen holding her coat over her head.

"Right," Parks said. "If the zoning changes tonight, the straw buyer executes the purchase."

Carol smiled at Easy and told herself to pay attention. She was paying attention. She could pay attention to fishermen and business both. It was all business now. She felt like Baxter bringing home a deal. She said to Parks, "So here's what we do. We go to the meeting and commit out loud to our plans for the plant. Then we pray the town council votes for our version of the future. I was hoping to wait a few more hours before we announced, but here we are. You and Annette and my instincts are the due diligence we get."

She listened to the rain become lighter against the tent of her coat, and she said, "I'm standing with Ezekiel Parsons and Buddy Taormina, who say they would bring us fresh fish if we had the plant. Could be the critical margin. I'll ask them to bring fishermen from the high school to this evening's meeting at the town hall."

Parks said, "You can believe Mathews won't have any fishermen on his team. I'll bring who I can. The women off the line. We want a crowd."

"I'll see you there, Dave."

She put the cell away, and as if she were Baxter laying things out, she said to Buddy and Easy, "If we can keep the fish zoning, either they go back into the fish business, or they walk away. I'm certain they'll walk away, which will mean we're in business."

The rain stopped, and she took her coat from them, and Buddy looked at her feet in the puddle. He said to her, "We can bring what's left of the working harbor people."

She said, "The other boats will want to work with us?"

He said, "You're looking at a big part of the fleet right here, the offshore fleet. But you bet."

Easy was looking at her as if he had a question. His clothes were wet from the rain. Baxter would think it was funny to say that people like Easy didn't know to come in out of the rain.

She said, "You have a question, Easy."

"I do."

Carol thought she knew what the question was, and if she was right, it was a serious question but a question in her strike zone. He wanted to know whether she was on the up-and-up.

She said, "If the zoning changes, Mathews—or whoever's buying for him—gets to buy the plant from Baxter Blume and gets it at the cheap industrial-harbor price even with the harbor zoning gone. Parks tells me it's a signed contract."

Carol looked to both Easy and Buddy, but she kept a particular eye on Easy. She was absolutely on the up-and-up, and she didn't want Easy to think otherwise.

She went on. "Under that contract, Baxter Blume only owns the old plant long enough to sell it at the cheap price, and Mathews gets to develop Marblehead, whatever that is, on harbor land he got for next to nothing. If the zoning does not change, and Mathews decides he doesn't want the plant as an actual fish plant, which is the only way he could use harbor-zoned land, then Baxter Blume still owns the plant, but they cannot then sell at the Marblehead development price, because the zoning prevents Marblehead development. Okay?"

Easy and Buddy both nodded. They got it.

Carol went on anyhow, to nail it down for them. "Mathews has first crack, and our hope is that the zoning doesn't change, that it stays harbor, and Mathews decides not to buy. Then the plant is worth what it's worth right now and no more than that. I'll give Baxter Blume a fair offer for the plant on that current value. I don't know whether Baxter Blume will let me buy the plant, but I'm pretty sure they will. If they do, I need you guys to bring me the fresh fish that I think could make the plant profitable."

She thought Easy must have understood as soon as she'd begun to explain herself.

"Sounds good to me," Buddy said.

Easy said, "Me, too."

Buddy said, "We'll see you there at Town Hall tonight," and he pulled open the door and climbed into his flatbed.

Easy was already walking off to his own truck, and Carol wanted to kiss him.

Walls of Names

Carol had gotten to her apartment after dark last night and left before dawn this morning. Now in the daylight of early evening, she registered things more clearly: a galley kitchen, a small living-and-dining room, and a half bathroom; upstairs was a full bath and the little bedroom under the pitch of the roof, on which she could hear rain starting up again.

Out the low back window beside the bed, she got her first view of an enclosed, overgrown little graveyard. Narrow houses backed onto it all the way around, other windows looking onto a hundred plain gravestones, some leaning, some broken over and covered with briar. Slender branches of saplings grew to the height of her window, and their unfurling buds danced a green haze in the rain. All these years as an undertaker, and this was her first actual graveyard posting.

By the time she left for the meeting at Town Hall, daylight was nearly gone, and the rain had stopped once more. She went in a direction away from the high school, between narrow houses that had once been white and were flush against one another and tight on the street. They had small windows in warping clapboard, and off the curb was a gallery of rusted American cars.

She was on her way to fight for her company, and in her head Baxter was asking if this was the company she wanted.

Baxter wouldn't want it. Baxter wouldn't go anywhere near Town Hall tonight. His voice in her head told her, "Don't go to this meeting, Carol. If anybody asks where you were, tell them you had an episode. You pick up a company in twenty-four hours? In an industry you know nothing about? With people you just met?"

He laughed as if it were genuinely funny. He was right. But she was going to do it anyway. Screw you, Baxter, Carol thought.

A tiny gray dog yapped and threw itself against a window beside her, and Carol smelled seaweed and iodine decay in the evening's near-dark, as if the ocean were breathing over Elizabeth Island.

She zigzagged around the peeling rear levels of a Unitarian parish hall that had rooflines of gulls weeping, and the houses on the street swelled to two- and three-family buildings in pastel vinyl siding with racer tricycles on the porches. She walked past the bays of the Elizabeth Island Fire Department and past the back of the library toward what could only be Town Hall, three stories of blackened brick with elaborate turrets that disappeared into night and mist. People streamed up the granite steps to the grim entry.

Carol climbed halfway up the steps to watch the parade. She put her hands behind her and leaned out of the way against the iron railing. Easy and Buddy Taormina might have already gone in, but she saw men like them from the afternoon meeting in the high school gym. In the gym, she'd heard the microphone language of American bureaucracy. Here on the steps of a New England town hall, the men and their wives spoke Italian and Portuguese.

She walked in with the last of the stragglers, all of whom followed the rest of the crowd up a bright stairwell.

Carol stopped to peer into the oak and linoleum dim of the long hallway that handled everyday town business. Departments were painted on the pebbled glass windows of wooden doorways. Taxes, Clerk, Permits, and then it was too dark to read more. Carol wished it was daytime and she had an everyday reason to go into the hallway, even if only to pay off her parking tickets. She wished she knew the girls in the clerk's office. She wished she lived in a town, in this town. By the time she turned and started up the stairs, she was alone.

And the stairwell was bright and wide enough that she was startled by the height opening above her.

More surprising, the walls of the stairwell, from the first step, were covered with lists of names.

Painted in small gold letters, the names, men's names, came in tight yearly bunches, chronologically. The most recent years were at the lowest step, with only a couple of names each year and not every year. Earlier and earlier years climbed the rest of the two full floors up the stairwell. Back fifteen and twenty years, there were consistently five or ten names. Back fifty years, as Carol went up the stairs, every year had twenty or thirty names. They couldn't be war dead, not every year. By the second-floor landing, every year, year after year, from the nineteen twenties back up into the mid–eighteen hundreds, the names numbered a hundred, even as many as three hundred, a year. The lists at the bottom of the stairs, the most recent years, had been full of Portuguese and Italian names. Carol saw Taormina more than once. Up higher and earlier, into the late eighteen hundreds, it was a big proportion of Italian names. Highest up the walls were the earliest years, and the names were Carpenters and Wheelwrights, Parsonses.

They had to be the names of fishermen from this harbor who had died at sea. Carol was amazed there could be so many. She was more amazed that the ones left could find the courage to keep going out year after year. She wondered what became of the wives and children.

Then, for the second time in a day, she looked into a large room and over the heads of a crowd on folding chairs. There was a balcony around three sides of the room, and above the balcony, the ceiling was as high as the gym had been but with the remains of ornate molding from which fluorescent lights hung. The windows along the sides of the room were wide and tall and elegant. The walls and balcony and ceiling were white, with some of the molding still gilt.

At the far end of the room, the town council sat at their line of brown, mismatched tables, and one of the councillors announced the sorts of procedural formalities that drive the public away so the persistent can have what they want. But the public was certainly here, and this time it included women. Would Mathews and the fat boys be here? No. They'd keep a good distance between themselves and their zoning bonanza.

Up behind the council was a stage and a large mural of Pilgrims and Indians, of an abundance of fish and the fishing industry rampant, of a town hall like this one surrounded by steeples on its hill above the harbor.

Someone behind Carol said, "Is it you? Of course it is you."

Carol turned around to a short woman, round with fat, who stood legs apart and hands on hips. The woman was older than Carol, and she looked at Carol and then down at herself, smiling at what a pair they made for, short and tall, fat and skinny. Her hair had gone to white, but she had black eyebrows. She wore black pants and a black smock, and she looked tough enough to mother a town like Elizabeth. Carol towered over the woman and yet, for the strangest instant, wanted to climb into her arms and be cradled.

The woman said, "Ezekiel Parsons wants everybody to call you Beauty, but I call people by real names. You are Carol, which Ignacio told me, along with the fact you have big hands. Big hands are useful hands. You are very welcome here, Carol."

Carol put her hands in her pockets.

Through the doors, one of the council was calling for quiet as past business was read, and Carol nodded to the woman that they should whisper. The woman held one large hand toward whatever was the business in there and dismissed it.

Carol, before she could stop herself, said, "You have big hands, too."

"Thank you. They are hands that have done work always. My name is Anna Rose Taormina. My Elizabeth Island Wives of the Sea have prayed for years to keep our harbor, and then this year we gave up. We lost faith, Carol, and I am ashamed of that, but now you are here, and together we will succeed."

Carol remembered Easy introducing Buddy. His name was Buddy Taormina. She said, "Are you Buddy's mother?"

"Yes. It is not your fault, but why Ignacio must be made into Buddy, I can never know. Call me Anna Rose. You'll see it on one of Ignacio's boats that was my husband's for many years. Twenty years ago, I organized the Wives of the Sea, and now I can talk to both senators. They know to return my telephone call. The senators in Washington, not the crooks in Boston. But you don't need the senators for this. My women are here tonight, and Ignacio and Ezekiel brought all the men from the waterfront who are still sober enough after the meeting with the fisheries commission."

"It was a good day for the fishermen."

"If we can land fresh catch again in Elizabeth and sell direct to a processor, it is a better day. Do you know anything about what we do? No matter. It is not hard as long as the fish are with us. And just the same, we don't ever again stop praying." She took hold of Carol's arm and led Carol into the meeting.

Our Dead

Town council meetings were not a usual part of Easy's life, and this was the first time he'd paid attention to the podium. It was old, square, dinged but solid, dangling a cord, looking like something that'd been stolen off the boat. It was to the side of the town councillors, in front of the stage and under the mural. Easy watched Carol set herself there behind the podium and hold the top of it with both hands. She looked over the crowd. She didn't look nervous exactly. It was a full house, and Easy didn't think anybody hated her yet, so that was good. Somewhere in town, of course, Mathews and his fat pals were hating her; Carol had apparently kicked them all out in her first five minutes. Easy looked at Carol and thought of that and started to laugh out loud until Buddy gave him an elbow.

Carol was bending her knees a bit, feet apart, back-and-forthing a bit foot to foot. That had to be good, getting ready for action. Easy worried about her. He wanted her to get what she wanted. He didn't care so much about what her fresh fish angle

meant for him; he'd be fine with or without. He didn't even much
care if he was fine, and hadn't cared much about anything since
Mississippi and Angie and the baby. He'd kept going because that
was who he was, fishing and a couple friends. He was surprised by
how much he liked Carol, who was tough and smart and smiled
some and didn't seem to mind him.

He and Buddy and Dave Parks and Buddy's mother, Anna
Rose, had spread the word and gotten a lot of the town here, but
Easy wondered if the town cared. The fish and the real waterfront
work in the harbor had been dying for twenty years anyhow.
Unless you had skills like Easy and Buddy, it'd all been as good as
dead for most of the last ten. If the town got a hotel on the old
plant site, if they got condominiums for rich people, that would
buy educations for everybody's kids, and restaurants and tourists.
The value of everybody's houses goes through the roof. Easy cared
about the harbor, but he figured most of the people who had
showed up tonight were just pretending for a few minutes, and
then they'd be ready to get on with it.

Carol stepped away from the podium. She stepped out in
front of the town council table and faced the town.

She looked around at everybody, meeting their eyes. She knew
what she was doing. It was a roomful of fish-town working people, brand new to her, and she seemed at home. Mostly at home.

He wished she didn't look like she was smelling something. All
Easy could smell was low tide that the evening air was breathing into
town. Nothing new in that—Easy loved the smell—but now she was
checking out around her like she might have to shout Fire. Everybody was noticing now. Hold on, Carol, Easy thought, it's going to
be all right. He wished he could run up, whisper, "This is what you
do for a living, Carol. This is what you were made for," as if he knew.

She stood alone there in front of Elizabeth Island in her dark suit, and her quiet (a sexy thing, quiet) was enough to keep him sitting along with everybody else, waiting for her to speak.

She looked over everybody's heads.

She said, "I smell the ocean."

She said it loud, or it sounded loud because it was so quiet in the room. She sure didn't have to be loud to be heard. Also, nobody besides her would be surprised to smell the ocean in Elizabeth, but nobody said that. It stayed quiet but for Carol, now that she was going.

She said, "I didn't see anyone climb the stairs with reverence, but those names on the walls of the stairwell up to this room, those must be the names of men from Elizabeth Island who died at sea. Isn't that right?"

That was one way to start. The whole room nodded, Easy, too, and all of a sudden, he wanted the rest of the room to go away so he could listen by himself.

Carol said, "Anna Rose. Do you have family on that wall?"

Buddy's mother stood up and said, "Yes, I do," and sat back down.

Carol said, "Easy, I saw Parsonses on the wall. Is that you?"

Easy couldn't help it. He wanted to tell her, right out loud, how pretty she was. Instead, he stood up and said, ashamed but all in, "No, that's not me, Ms. MacLean. That's my family on the wall, but Easy Parsons is right here, alive still, and that's what I'm hoping to stay."

Everyone laughed, and he sat down, afraid to look and see if she hated him.

She was quiet, and he peeked. She didn't look pissed. She looked ready to go again. Maybe he'd been useful, which was all, until now, he'd wanted since he left Mississippi.

She said, "I'd be curious to know how many of you do have family or connections of one kind or another on that wall, how many of you knew the people behind the most recent sets of names. Would you forgive me if I asked you to stand up?"

Easy got himself up quick, but so did the rest of the room. A working fish-town in its bones, all of them stood. Easy knew them all, except Carol, and Carol belonged here even though she was pretty. Everybody else—him, too, obviously—was a long way from pretty. The men were lumps or withering or broken in half, from jobs that ate your body. Most of them also didn't care so much about shaving. The drinkers, men and women both, it was in their faces. The druggers, a few had come, the old ones, which you never expected at first but you weren't going to mistake them; they'd have come because they knew they had a connection in the crowd. The women didn't look a hell of a lot different, though there were Asian and South American women who had showed up mostly without their men. All the women's hair, long and short, looked ratty, only some on purpose. There was muscle on some of the women and fat on some, though not so much of the fat. Working women, and they'd popped out kids. A couple of the women had been pretty as girls, he knew from firsthand viewing, and he would never tell them they'd changed even if in high school they'd told him it was a good thing he could do this or that because otherwise he was a mirror-breaker. What was best about this ugly crowd, though, was they dressed great. Biggest clothing store in town was work clothes, and that store was on hard times with everybody else. The men's shirts in the room here were torn or lost their color or both and the jeans and the khakis bagged in the knees and the ass. A few— the sharks that sold summer real estate and whatnot—they wore cheap, well-pressed, nice clothes, but if somebody like Easy knew they were cheap clothes, believe it. The women—how was it they all wore secondhand? Who got the new dresses? Easy looked at everybody, and he liked them, even the assholes, of which there were plenty, himself too now and then. He wasn't going to make out that he liked himself. He wasn't brought up to say that, and he'd felt different too many times. But he didn't mind saying he was proud to be one of these people. He'd stand up for the people out on the wall and for the people still breathing in here both.

Carol said, "I can feel the floor beneath my feet move as if it is floating out of sight of land, and I smell the ocean as if it waits outside the doors of this room with the dead of your harbor, your dead, the men of Elizabeth Island who died doing what it is that the people of Elizabeth Island do. The ocean scares me more than most of you could imagine, but if I lived here, I would not want that harbor to go to condominiums for rich folks from someplace else. I would not want it to go to a hotel for tourists. And I don't hate rich folks or tourists. I wish I were a rich tourist myself."

That got a bit of a laugh, and not just from Easy. She was funny, Carol MacLean.

She said, "I'm as much a stranger here as any tourist, and you can tell me to go away, but I'm going to say this. What could you have been thinking? How could you imagine letting your harbor go? That harbor is who you are. That harbor, that working harbor, is the soul of this place. Lose it, and you lose yourself. If the economics are not working, then you have to change the economics, on your own terms. You have to be who you are in new ways, ways that honor the ocean in this room and all these names of men on whom all of us float right this minute."

She stopped, and the room was quiet and stayed quiet. She wasn't even from here and she'd opened up the heartbreak of the town. He'd tried to be funny about his family, and she'd opened him up.

She stood where she was like she was waiting for somebody else to say something, but nobody was raising their hand.

She said, "If you decide to keep your harbor zoning, I will buy and run the old plant."

Then she did walk away, far off to the side, and the room stayed silent. Easy watched her standing against one of the high windows out to the night and away from the room's main light. For the shadow where she stood, and for being himself halfway to bawling, he could not see her clearly, but she was beautiful. She was beautiful because of who she was and what she just did. She was also brave as hell, and that included having been put to her knees from a phone call, which he would never mention.

One of the councilmen coughed into a mike, and Anna Rose Taormina stood and pointed at him and said, "Shut up."

Then Anna Rose turned around looking at everybody. She knew them like Carol couldn't possibly, and they knew her. Easy loved her. She had welcomed him back from the delta and told him to pull his oar. Now she said to everybody, as she kept turning and watching them, "If you think we should keep the harbor zoned for harbor work, stand up."

Easy stood with the rest of the town, and Anna Rose pointed at the councillor with the mike and said, "Okay, now you can talk. Say that the harbor zoning regulations stay as they are, resolved unanimously, and then be sure the secretary's got it down in the minutes. I can't hear you."

Everybody laughed, the councillor, too, and so did the secretary as she wrote. Easy watched Carol by her black window. He thought she might be thinking of all the work that lay ahead. It would be a lot of work. He didn't think she'd be afraid of that, and by the time she walked out of the shadow, she had her business face on solid. She was ready to work. She was everything he'd thought she was and more.

What Now?

Carol took her time making her way through the crowd. She was shy, now, around them. She was so used to delivering bad news.

"You. Ichabod."

A guy in a new chambray shirt shouted it, at her obviously. He had to be Mathews's agent at the meeting. He'd worn the shirt to look one-with-the-people when he talked about the new hotel or whatever was to be the development, though he'd never even stood up when Anna Rose Taormina asked. Carol guessed he was going to take a swing at her to justify his evening.

She had been called Ichabod more than once, and by the time she figured out what it meant, it hadn't bothered her. But now she was on her own and was open to scrutiny on her own account. What was more, this was not just about her. She had declared a responsibility to Elizabeth Island and the people who surrounded her. She needed to stand into that right now and face whatever Chambray was going to say. She got up on the seat of a chair next to Anna Rose Taormina, so Chambray and everybody else could get a good look at her. The meeting was done, but people who were leaving stopped.

"What now, Ichabod?" Chambray said.

"Now we go to work," she said and hoped that would be it and knew it wouldn't. He'd been beaten, and he didn't like being beaten. He knew how smart she wasn't, that Baxter Blume wouldn't send a heavyweight out to bury a company the size of Elizabeth's Fish. He thought he knew she was all bluff, which could turn out to be the case, but the rest of the room should not think it. She believed in herself and believed in the old plant. Starting right this minute, she believed that she lived here.

He said, "You're going to work that plant? What the hell do you know about fish? How about giving us all a glimpse of what makes you think you can turn a profit from an antique operation that industry experts couldn't make a go of? You just killed these people's chance to turn their harbor into a revenue source again, and I want to know, just out of curiosity, what a small-time corporate undertaker can do to replace that revenue. Is Baxter Blume going to help you out? Do they have the faintest idea what you're up to?"

That was it, wasn't it? Carol thought. She had not just said she was going to do something, upon which people would depend. She had offered the hope of a lot of hard work. She knew what the work was, essentially, but she'd never specifically done it. She was scared shitless that she would not be able to do it well enough.

Baxter wandered through the inside of her head with his hands in his pockets. He said, "Okay, you're here, and you're naked. Ignore it. First thing you learn in boarding school. So what if you had an episode and ended up without any clothes on? Say, My clothes are on. Say, I have great clothes and you don't have any idea what I'm doing and it's none of your business. Say, I've caught you red-handed and I'm going to call the FBI and get to the bottom of this."

Carol smiled at Chambray, beamed at him, but Chambray had lost a deal, and he wasn't going to back off for a smile. He said, "You got your zoning. You killed off a lot of potential business in this town, business this town needs. Now what, Ichabod?"

Carol said, "I'm going to work, and I'm bringing as many people with me as I can, real work that's a real part of this town. What's your business plan, pal? Your people, whoever they are, as if we didn't know, wanted to buy the site of the old fish plant at a harbor zoning price and then sell to Marriott or a condo developer at Marblehead prices. So who was supposed to get that bonanza? Your fat-boy employers, who've already ripped the town off and driven Elizabeth's Fish into the sea? And the continuing revenue goes to a corporate holding company a thousand miles away, while the folks in this room get to be the waiters and the maids. Have I got that right?"

Chambray was already headed out with his briefcase and his thousand-dollar raincoat, and Carol shouted after him, "Have I got that right?"

Baxter would have drawn blood, but Carol had managed it cleanly. She was surprised to realize it had been fun.

⅄

Soon everyone was gone but Dave Parks, Annette Novato, Anna Rose Taormina, Buddy Taormina, and Easy Parsons. Parks said, "What now, Carol?"

It wasn't Chambray's tone of voice, but the words reverberated in the empty room, and Carol had to answer them for her team.

She started for the doors, saying, "Let's go down to the old plant and orient."

Easy was beside her when they got to the stairs. She wondered if that was on purpose. The stairs were wide, so he wasn't pushed against her, and she didn't look at him, but she felt him there. Now that the meeting was done, she wanted to get into bed by herself next to her graveyard. She wanted to be alone under the covers and let herself be as afraid as she was of Chambray's questions. Yet here Easy was, with all the feelings of the parking lot, and she was afraid of that, too.

She went fast down the stairs, running away to get her plant in gear, her own plant. She wasn't too tired for that. But so did Easy go fast, right beside her. And with that, that quickly, she could have been a girl, the two of them skipping down stairs hard as they could but not away from anything. For fun. She could have laughed.

Outside, she walked fast along the night-lit street that ran in front of Town Hall, and she knew Easy would stay with her. She watched him in glances. His arms were long and they swung, and his body lunged with every step. He angled forward. He covered ground. She walked faster. So did he, and they pulled away from the others like they wanted to be by themselves, the kind of thing girls in the parking lot did, and she'd done with Dominic, that long ago and not since.

As they passed the YMCA, Easy said, "That asshole with his Ichabod thing. I got to tell you, I almost broke him down."

Carol looked at him when he said that, but he didn't look back. He meant it, and he would know how to punch somebody out. She didn't believe that kind of stuff was important to him, any more than it was to her, and just the same, he was telling her everything. He'd brought them to his truck, and he opened her door and shoved rain gear and mail and two cell phones mostly out of the way, and she climbed in. She smelled sweat and grease, and she fit her feet around the extra pair of boots he had on her side of the floor. She tried to remember the last time she had been this nervous in a car with a man.

Forty-plus years ago, Dominic took Carol out in her bent Mustang before her dad got it straightened. She was thirteen. They went to the dirt behind the old fabricator buildings. Dominic put the seat all the way back and had her sit between his legs. She took it high into second and sat back against him, and he didn't touch the wheel, but he wrapped around her with his hands there in case. Nobody else, just them and her fishhook of a Mustang. When she had her speed, he shouted, "Now!" She hit the brake so hard she drove herself back into him, and she ripped the wheel and held it. She didn't care if she died. She stood on the brake and ripped the wheel and was going to hold on, like he'd said, the full nine yards to hell. They lifted and stayed up on two wheels, and he laughed the weird squeal he did when regular laughing wasn't enough. They settled and slid, and he shouted, "Step on it!" She stood on the gas and they spun. That Mustang she'd tricked, it spun like a top, Dominic squealing and her not making a sound. She stayed planted on the gas and kept the wheel locked over and they spun, and she could feel his heart hammering against her bony back through their T-shirts and his smell of grease and sweat.

Only this was a three-quarter-ton flatbed, a truck she could like but different from the Mustang. And this was Easy beside her, and he didn't say anything, and neither did she. It was only a minute down to the harbor and the plant. By the time Easy got out his side and she got out hers, everybody else had arrived, and Carol had to come up with a plan.

They gathered in the dark next to the fence, and she said, "Please take a moment here to let things sink in. And excuse me. I'm going to take my moment on the dock. Right back."

She opened the fence instead of sliding under and walked out through the tunnel beneath the offices that closed the overhead gap between buildings.

She got to the dock and looked down the water side of the plant for the extruded rails of sliding doors. She said aloud to herself, "What now?" She said, "Come on." She didn't know what now, but she knew that it was there to be had. She waited as if the knee-jerk instinct Baxter valued might swim up out of the slack black water beneath her.

Instead, she heard someone walking out the tunnel.

It was Easy.

She pointed across at the darkened silhouette of his boat and said, "A hundred feet?" as if she knew about boats.

"Ninety-two," he said, and he was it, of course. Easy was it.

She said, "You're my business plan. I almost forgot."

He said, "You did great tonight."

She grabbed his shoulders and pulled herself against him and kissed him. His shoulders were strong, and he kissed her back, and his lips were softer than she would have thought. She'd meant, if she'd meant anything, to kiss him and run away. She kissed him longer. They stopped and he smiled. He was the one who tilted his head to the side for everyone else waiting on the other side of the plant. She was supposed to be the businessman. She kissed him once more and laughed before she ran.

Jessop

As long as nobody was taking advantage, Dave Parks had always liked to see an office romance, but this was the first time he'd seen one without there being an office yet.

Carol came hurrying out from the tunnel and through the gate in the fence, and as she came, she yelled a little too loud, "It's the fresh fish." That was a good thing to yell at the moment, but Dave wasn't so far removed from Blueberry Hill that he couldn't tell when there'd been kissing.

Give her credit, though; she didn't look back when Easy Parsons followed her out at a discreet distance.

Everybody stood in a huddle there at the fence, and Carol stepped into the huddle like a quarterback. She said, "Also, we move our offices downstairs and lease out the office space upstairs. But it's the fresh fish that's going to give us our margins."

Anna Rose said, "Of course it is the fresh fish."

Dave was not going to smile away any secrets, but it looked

like Carol was having difficulty not smiling. She had her lips pressed together, but the corners of her mouth were tipping up just the same.

Easy said, "It's not just that Carol's doing fresh."

Was Carol blushing? Who could tell in the dark?

Easy said, "It'll be nice to bring in fresh on any scale around here for the first time in ten years. But the thing is, Carol's going to get her fish at a better price. All the other producers buy through one of the auctions now, and that means they have to pay the auction fee and then pay to bring the fish to where they're going to cut it. Carol doesn't have to do any of that, because me and Buddy'll sell and deliver to her door. More than that, she'll get full discount of whatever our costs would be in time and fuel if we had to drive our boats down to the nearest auction and back. Carol's going to get a volume of fish cheaper than anybody between Connecticut and Maine. She just has to cut it and sell it."

Well said, Dave thought, and good to have Easy say it. He was a smart guy, and everybody on the harbor respected him, despite the fact he could be more reserved than the Old Man of the Mountain. Carol was not your socializing sort either, at first glance, though she did have the smile she was concealing.

Buddy said, "There are still cutters in town. That's no problem."

Carol said, "Anna Rose, I'm thinking you and the Elizabeth Island Wives of the Sea are how we sell our fresh fish."

Anna Rose Taormina looked like she'd been waiting years for the proposition, and she probably had, and Dave was embarrassed nobody in the old company had ever thought of it. They wouldn't have had product for her, but even so.

She said, "We call it The Elizabeth Island Wives of the Sea Bring You the Freshest Fish You Ever Tasted in Your Life."

It was perfect Anna Rose, and not a bad name, and Dave laughed.

"Don't laugh," Anna Rose said. "It is a good name, and we know places and we know people. People and places know who we are. All the way in Worcester, they know. In Springfield, they know. These fishermen only hope in their dreams they can bring more fish than I and my women will sell."

"No," Dave said, making himself serious for Anna Rose. "No, it's a good name, and you're right about it working."

He said to Carol, "Part of me still thought we were kidding, but if we buy our frozen block fish at market and make and sell our fish sticks at cost, we can be competitive. The fresh fish sideline, if we're buying under market from Easy and Buddy, there's our profit margin."

Carol said, "Thanks, Dave," and looked him in the eye and nodded, making a connection beyond just polite. She wanted his confirmation for herself and for the rest of them, and he was glad to give it and glad of the appreciation.

Carol said to the others, "Does everybody get that? Assuming the lines here still run for our basic fish stick, the fresh fish that Easy and Buddy and other boats bring in will give us the profit margins that will give us a chance. Leasing the offices will give us another boost."

Dave watched her willing herself to believe what she said. And why not? Though he wondered whether Baxter and Blume would believe it.

Now Carol turned to Annette. "What else would help us on costs, Annette? What are you seeing over there in the new offices that we don't want around our necks here?"

Annette said, "Aside from that electricity I told you about, the new plant is paying on debt. If we don't have anything to spare, we don't want to carry debt on our plant."

Carol looked at Dave. She wanted him to break the news. "What does that mean, Dave, about the debt?"

This was the big play for her, Dave thought. Nobody wanted to use their own money in business, but if you were going to the edge, you went with your own money. She looked like she had a sense of humor about it, but there wasn't anything funny about it for Dave. Sure, if you used your own money, every dollar coming in the door was yours. But if nothing came in, how funny was that? She was tougher than Dave, no question about it.

He said to everybody, "It means we buy our plant for cash money," and he hoped all of them would run for their cars as he ran for his. Because no way were the contributions of most of the employees of the plant going to fund a stock ownership plan for this plant. He said it anyway, asked Carol, "ESOP?"

Carol said, "ESOP?" and smiled around at all of them. Dave wondered if there was a more special smile for Easy Parsons.

Dave said, "I'm almost to retirement. Can't we please borrow?" Which, okay, he followed with a laugh, and a gesture to their beat-up old plant. What did you do, if you weren't going to run? You laughed. His two girls, back in Pittsburgh, were out of school and married to guys making more than him, and his wife, here, Barbara, had all the courage she'd ever need. Dave was the worrier, and he didn't want Barbara to have to tighten her belt for him at this late stage of the game.

Everybody looked at the plant with Dave. It was a wet night. They would have to decorate some if they wanted to lease the offices.

Carol said, "Dave, if anybody would loan on it, what kind of rate would they give us?"

His turn again. "We maintained the lines," he said. "They're ugly but they run. We can find somebody who'd lend. But no, we're not going to get any sweetheart rates until we prove what the business will do. And until then, we can't afford to give away any dollars that come in the door. Shit."

It was raining again, and the fence gleamed and so did the walls of the plant and the corrugations of the lobster company going back toward town. The rain silvered down through the security lights. Dave thought for no good reason except hope that Carol might now decide she wanted to kiss Easy again, and everybody else could go home.

Instead, she kicked him, Dave. She said, exactly like he knew she was going to do, "Even an ESOP is not enough, Dave."

"What?" he said. "My life savings aren't enough? You want my kids?" He shoved his chin out, opened his hands in disbelief, and got a laugh from everybody.

Anna Rose said to him, "It was from my girls I had to put up with that kind of attitude, David. They wanted drama. The boys just sneaked. With the boys, I never knew until the hospital called, or the police."

Carol said, no break in focus, "We'll get a fire-sale price from Baxter Blume, and even so, we'll need more money than what we can get from ourselves and our employees."

Annette would have heard of it, but Dave said to Easy and Anna Rose and Buddy, "Employee stock ownership plan. That's what we're talking about with the ESOP."

Easy said, "No, Dave. Teesop."

Dave said, "*E*, actually. ESOP."

"Teesop. I'm talking a *t*."

Dave pointed a finger at Easy and said, "*T* for town stock ownership plan. I knew that. Teesops."

Buddy said, "Sell stock in this plant to regular people in town?"

Anna Rose said, "Why not? I live in town, and if I had been running this company, it wouldn't look like this and nobody would have made that Disney's World in the woods. Families still have money in this town. Fishing families. Harbor families."

Carol said, "Do you think people will want to do it?"

Dave's question was, How did Carol learn to drive this bus this well after one day in town, after a lifetime of killing things?

"Don't you worry about wanting," Anna Rose said. "Everybody, and a lot of them wasn't at the meeting, have been waiting for tonight. Maybe they're already at my house with money. If they aren't I will take you to their kitchens and you will tell them."

Buddy Taormina said, "Ma. We want to be sure we sell something that works. Take your time, Ma."

Dave settled in to watch this play out. He also resolved it was time for a new raincoat.

Easy said, "It ain't us selling, Buddy. It's us buying. It's Beauty selling to us and to everybody else."

So he did call her Beauty. Dave hadn't believed it.

Anna Rose said, "Ezekiel Parsons, you sound like cold feet."

Easy stared at his feet and said, "Thank you."

Carol smiled at Easy when he looked up. Dave saw Easy smile, too. Easy was ready to invest, regardless of the cold feet. Dave watched as Carol kept looking at Easy, and she didn't let the smile go away, and Easy didn't let his go away either.

For Buddy, Carol got serious.

She said, "Buddy's got a point. We want to go inside at daylight with somebody who can persuade us that at least the mechanics work. That may not be all Buddy wants to know, but it's a start. Who was running things here while the head of production was eating off the new plant?"

"He was there tonight," Dave said. "Ben Garcia. He's a kid, but he can run this place with his eyes closed. And he maintained it."

"We need him down here first thing in the morning. I need to see it go, and Buddy needs to see it go. And if we can, we also need to dig out some numbers on this plant alone. Annette, can we show people that it was breaking even when it was still running?"

Carol was asking in public for a projection that would have consequences for her neighbors. Annette was frozen, and Carol said, "Anything you can pull, Annette, the best glimpse you can manage. What about the cursory numbers you ran for the fat boys when they were pretending they wanted to sell it?"

"Oh, that's right." Annette unfroze. "With anything recent, every figure refers to another figure and another figure in a circle, on purpose. Still, yes, like we said."

Everybody looked at Annette as if they thought she was going to fall down, but Annette, if you gave her a minute, was always fine. She looked around at everybody and, perfectly solid, said, "Okay, Ms. MacLean. Carol."

Buddy said, "Those assholes. Excuse me, Mr. Parks."

Dave raised his hands to Buddy, no foul, and guessed that it must be sweet for Carol to come into a town and not be the rat.

She said, "We'll use what you find, Annette, and hope it gives us a fair grip on our chances. While we're at that, we'll also get ready to sell shares. I'll find someone to set up the plan. Then, Anna Rose, you and I will go to the kitchens."

Carol is driving the bus, Dave thought, and picking up speed.

To Buddy, Carol said, "We don't sell a share to anyone until we believe people can get a fair understanding of our chances. There will be risk, no matter what, and we'll say so. But we'll know the equipment runs, and we'll have a good argument for running it. Even in the best scenario, it's going to be a risk, and not an ordinary risk, so before I ask anybody else, I'll put in more of my own money than I can afford to lose. I'll put myself as much as or more at risk than anyone else who comes in."

Everyone waited for her to go on, but that was it for now, thank God.

Dave knew he was going to have to kick in. Maybe it would feel like fun in the morning.

Carol said, "Let's all go home. Dave, unless we hear differently, we'll meet your engineer here at eight thirty."

It was too late and too wet for a postmortem, but as people went for their cars, Dave got Carol's eye and gave her a thumbs-up. One day at a time, and today was the first of a whole hell of a lot of days, God willing, and just the same, it had been a hell of a day. Carol had definitely scored. If Dave was going to make a fool of himself with his money, which he was, at least he'd be doing it for an honest, good cause, which was one feel-good way to lose your money, and he'd be working with a woman who had juice and smarts. All in all, Dave felt good.

Then there was Easy, standing by the passenger door of his truck, waiting for Carol. Carol was standing still with her fists up under her chin, looking like a child on the first day in a new school, the first minute on the playground. Now Dave, if he were going to be scared, which was what Carol looked (if you could believe that), he'd be scared about everything that had happened today and was going to happen as a result—the business part. In fact, he was scared. What he would never be scared about was going to sit next to someone he wanted to kiss, especially if that someone wanted to kiss him. A theoretical question, not involving wives. Admittedly, kissing Easy Parsons would, for Dave, be a drag.

He watched Carol watching Easy wait by his truck, Easy watching back. Inside his head and damn near out loud, Dave said, "Oh, come on, Carol. Go. Please. He's a good person and so are you, and these things don't happen so much after you turn fourteen."

She shook her head at Easy. It looked like a nice shake from where Dave stood, but there it was, a shake, a no, and Easy probably understood that Carol wasn't a waffler.

She turned and said to Dave, "I'm going to walk."

Fun

Baxter's Greenwich phone rang at two thirty in the morning. He got up, closing the bedroom door behind him so Josie wouldn't have to listen, and took the call in the upstairs study. It was Carol MacLean, and Baxter's first assumption was that something catastrophic had happened. Second assumption: she was in another time zone. He remembered she was just up the coast with her fish, and he wondered if Remy had told her.

He said, "Carol, are they shooting at you?" What Baxter did for a living was still fun, two thirty or not, and truth be told, he could still go longer than the kids.

She said, "I want some going-away presents." Apparently Remy had told her. Knowing Carol, however, Baxter believed she would nonetheless bury his fish plant responsibly. He waited to hear what it was she wanted.

She let him wait. Carol had never called him at home before, and Baxter imagined her sitting on the edge of her latest rent-a-bed.

He said, "Carol, I wish I hadn't told you to get lost, and I never should have thrown the Beast thing at you. I should have just told you that you were out."

He assumed she would recognize that as twice notable for him. Speaking first, and almost apologizing. He offered this as a way to start the negotiation for whatever it was she wanted.

She said, "Yep." A new word for her, one she'd learned from him, if he wasn't mistaken. Next thing you knew, she'd be coming back at him with "no sweat," except "no sweat" was forgiving, and he didn't sense forgiveness was her mind-set at the moment.

He said, "Blume liked Susannah, and he built you out. I could have argued, but he had something I wanted. You might not think that what I traded you for was what you're worth, but there it is."

He didn't think she would ask what he'd traded her for. He said, "What I traded you for was free time. I'm stepping back from the new fund, which is what Blume ought to do, and that means assholes get to shoot at what I'm not around to stick up for. Sometimes they shoot for the hell of it. I thought I'd made it clear how good you were, but it wasn't clear enough."

Carol was still silent. Baxter liked her more by the minute, and he'd always liked her. He could never understand why nobody else saw as much in her as he did. He hoped her room was not god-awful. He wondered if it was raining up there.

He said, "I promised Blume not to tell you until you'd buried the fish, so I tried to get it across without telling you, in so many words, that we didn't want you, that we were assholes, that obviously we were never going to put you into your own company."

And that was just about his limit. Baxter was an absolute never-complain-never-explain man, unless he was dickering with other deal makers, in which case it was anything that worked.

At the moment Carol was a deal maker. It was going to be a tiny deal, but Baxter was delighted to be dealing, and in the middle of the night, and dealing with Carol of all people.

Just to be sure she was on the right page, he said, "But then you patronized me with authoritative comme il faut spleen and left the room like somebody who wanted her company and was ready to take it. That made me realize I hadn't gotten the message across, so I told Remy what was up and told him to tell you. So screw Blume. Blume got Susannah. He got to push you out of the plane just because I liked you. He got enough of what he wanted, and you're not going to rip us off just because we didn't give you the company you wanted and then fired you."

"So you participated in the good deed? It wasn't just Remy?"

Finally, a voice. "Carol. Admittedly I told him what was up for a number of reasons. But he also knew you weren't supposed to know. I told him to go ahead and tell you. He's a serious friend for you, and believe it or not, so am I."

"Truth be told, Baxter, you took back the company you promised me, and then you fired me."

She was right, but Baxter was saddened to hear Carol say it. He thought of her as a special case, less deserving of untruths. On the other hand, when it was necessary, lying happened. He said, "You aren't going to rip us off, are you, Carol?"

She said, "Here it is."

"All right. But first tell me you're not going to rip us off. I'd hate for Blume to be right on that."

"No, I'm not. Though the CEO, the CFO, the heads of production and of marketing at the fish, they ripped the Germans off in building the new plant, and the Japanese looked the other way. What I want to do is buy the old plant and run it myself. The bad guys had set up a last game to buy the old plant cheap and get zoning changed for a hotel. You could not have kept the property yourself if the zoning change went through. They would have gotten it, and gotten that hotel money. I killed the zoning change tonight, and they won't want to buy now. I'll beat their old offer and anyone else's offer. Probably nobody else will offer. I think I can make it work. It's not worth your while to make it work. You do not want it. Send Remy to do the burial on the new plant and the debt. Tell him to make the best deal he can with me."

A one-day plunge was nothing he hadn't done himself, occasionally, once even with his own money. He suspected Carol would be going in, maybe all in, with her own money. If it had been anyone besides Carol, with her skills and drive, he would have been surprised she hadn't broken out sooner. "You've been busy, Carol," he said.

When he first met her, she was taking a summer course on field sales management, a continuing-ed thing for grunts put on by the Harvard Business School. Baxter and a couple of biz school guys he'd known in ROTC took the course out of curiosity, which was instantly satisfied, except for Carol, the only woman, there in her three identical suits, taking furious notes and watching the real business school guys as if they were from another planet, which of course they were, among those line salesmen. She introduced herself like it was an act of abject courage. In turn, to prepare for the final exam, he took her and his buddies out along the Charles so she could lecture them on what happened in all the classes they missed. They had fun at that, and after each session, they asked her to dinner, and she ran away as fast as she could to avoid jinxing the fun she already had in the bag. Never occurred to her that, aside from Baxter himself, she was the most interesting person in their little group. And yes, he followed her one evening, because he knew she was staying in a dormitory on the business school side of the river, and yet after the sessions she often headed into the Yard. When she stopped and, in what looked like a ceremony, put her hand on a corner of one of those brick insane-asylum buildings, he crept close enough to hear her say, "I am at Harvard, Dad." Baxter didn't laugh about stuff like that. He respected it, and he understood that it would take a while before Carol knew she was more than Harvard. It occurred to Baxter that he would be smart to hire her one day.

On his phone tonight in Greenwich and on hers in her fish neighborhood, Carol said, "I haven't unloaded any assets from the new plant, and I think you'll want to just empty the box, but if I take the old plant, that means you've gotten good value out of my time. Remy may be able to sell all the new production hardware as a package. He'll figure it out. He can get his feet wet."

"That's funny, Carol. Get his feet wet. In the fish business. Is this a going-away present? Am I giving you the old plant?"

"I'm buying the old plant, and paying fair value, and saving you time and trouble."

"Okay. What's the favor?"

She went quiet, but now it was her play. He waited for real. He was genuinely curious. He'd always been expecting Carol to surprise, and here she was.

She said, "I want you to send somebody who will set up a stock plan for us. It would be tough for us to get loans on the old plant, and any loans would be expensive, so I'm going to try and get the employees and the town to pitch in. I think they will. I want you to do this for free and tell yourself that it's part of the price of getting rid of the plant. Send up one of Patterson's good numbers and have him put it together and run it through your machinery so we can give it as a turnkey package for someone up here to manage. It'll be tiny and a pain in the ass that way, but a big help to us. Also I'd like it if Remy chased the old executive team a little to keep them off my ass. He may even want to chase them for real, but that's probably not worthwhile."

She finished and Baxter was amused and pleased.

He hoped she felt as good as she ought to.

That said, it would be unseemly to roll over immediately. He pushed a little. "Why would I do all this, Carol?"

"Because you can do it so much more quickly and easily and cheaply than I can."

"You're a late bloomer, Carol, but you're blooming. Congratulations. Now, tell me again why I'd want to do those things."

"Because you owe me."

"You worked hard. I paid you. In fact, when I brought you on board you never asked for a salary, and I gave you a fair one. You still get a fair one. I've had a fair severance drawn up for your welcome home party."

She said, "Baxter."

She didn't have to remind him. Baxter never forgot a chit. Though he didn't mind if one was never called.

"For fun," he said. "Remind me."

"Aside from the broken promise of a company and getting fired? Okay, two things."

"The broken promise and the firing were largely out of my control. And I'm not positive there are other things, Carol."

He listened to the silence and hoped she was not deciding to give him the benefit of the doubt. She had to know he enjoyed haggling over a nickel, even if there was no question he would send Remy and put someone on her plan. He would also check it all out himself.

She said, "First, I tutored you and your two Navy buddies beside the Charles River for several days one summer. Remember that? At the time, you told me you owed me, and I don't care what you—"

"I remember. I didn't need the tutoring any more than I needed the class, but we had a good time, and that counts. What else?" He knew what she meant, and he knew it had been a lousy thing. But it had not come from him. On that count, he was innocent.

"At the end of the summer, you pinned a big piece of paper on my back that said 'Beast.' That's the second thing you owe me for."

"Nope."

"Not you?"

"No."

Baxter wasn't sure she believed him, and it had been such a rotten name for her to get stuck with that he felt guilty even though he hadn't been the one to give it. After their driver's-license test of a final exam, he and his buddies had picked Carol up under the arms and walked her over the bridge and bought her shorts and a summer top and espadrilles and sat her down to drink pitchers of beer outside across from the revered brick. Then they walked to the river and shouted something and walked back and had ice cream. They finished up in a bar that might have been in a basement where Carol told them in insufficient detail about her alley and her career selling parts, and when Baxter and his pals talked about a destroyer, she identified, from inside, by the sound of a passing muffler, the kind of muffler, the model and year of car, and in astonishing detail what had been done to its engine and almost certainly to its suspension. When they got her back to her dorm, she went down to her knees to throw up, and one of his buddies said, "Beauty down." Baxter bent to the eternal crouch, holding back the hair and steadying the head, and the other asshole said, "No, it's a beast down."

There was never any paper pinned on her, but that "beast down" asshole saw one of the salesmen the next day and told the story to try to make friends across the class divide. From there, history.

Baxter had never said it until Carol's last visit to the offices, when he tried to tell her she was out, and he hadn't liked saying it even then.

He wasn't going to go through all of that now. He said, "Carol, you occupy a unique and blessedly bright place in my universe of ambivalences. I like you. I value you, and I always have, and I would not lie about something like this. It's not a lie I'd want to carry around."

"Okay," she said. "The first thing is still enough."

"The first thing is enough," he said.

"Thank you."

"You're welcome. Also, Carol, I appreciate you not kicking me in the nuts over my promise of a company. I would have done it if I could."

A laugh here would have been fair, but silence again. "Good-bye" would have been a disappointing understatement, but after all, she'd gotten what she came for. She stayed silent on the phone.

It was going on three o'clock.

He said, "Carol?"

"Yes."

"Blume is trying not to die, and he's got so many pills to take it's hard to tell which one has ruined him. But he liked you. There's nobody home now, but he liked you."

"Thanks."

"What's more, this is the best thing that could happen to you. You're ready, and killing all those picked-over orphan companies was about to eat you up. This is the nick of time. You should have a company to run."

She asked, and here was maybe what she'd been waiting to say. He should have said it first, but maybe it was better she asked so it didn't come from him gratuitously. He could be gratuitous.

She said, "Can I do it?"

He put spine and fire in his voice and said, "Of course you can do it. You've been able to do it for years. I've been hanging on to you because I run a good deal until I can't run it anymore. All it needed was you getting canned and deciding you wanted to grab a company for yourself. If I weren't getting old and soft, I would steal it back from you, because it's probably a good company."

"It's way too small for you."

It was an awkward conversation, and he was glad to have gotten it out of the way. He wasn't sure about going back to bed. He knew that he was going to miss Carol. He told her, "It is way too small. I wish you luck with your fish. Be happy, Carol. Have fun. You've got a company."

Management

Baxter was a manager, among other things. He found people like Carol and got them to do what he needed done. Carol would have to be a manager now, and she needed to find her people. Dave Parks was solid. Annette seemed like a solid person, but she was still finding her way out of her old responsibilities into her new and much larger ones.

There was no way Carol was getting back to sleep. She needed to get Annette in motion. She felt badly about waking her and called anyway.

Annette answered on the third ring, and Carol said, "I'm sorry it's so early, but Baxter Blume's sending a guy up to replace me and another guy to organize our stock offering. We need to do as much digging as we can before they get here. The fat boys' straw buyer made a supposedly reasonable offer based on the cursory price projections you got up. What I'm hoping is that there are other footprints in the snow surrounding those projections. I mean any facts, however far removed, that are relevant to the projections. If there are, and they undermine the projections, we need to know. Any supporting evidence lost in corners, well, wouldn't that be nice. Okay?"

"I have it all, Ms. MacLean."

"Carol's fine."

"No, I have it all."

"You have it all?"

"I built that price for the plant, using asset and operation summaries, but Mr. Mathews didn't want anything too detailed. The odd thing was that some information seemed to be missing, which was part of why I said figures went in circles. I've never been in charge of the overall financial picture. I manage accounts and I've been around a long time, but I've never seen everything. My price projection was as much of everything as I'd ever seen at one time. Then Dave and I found the sales agreement, answering my pricing, in Mr. Mathews's private file cabinet. But tonight, after we left the old plant, I went back to the new plant, and in Mr. Mathews's file cabinet found evidence that, like you're asking, the plant is worth more than my projections or the purchase offer."

Annette is coming right along, Carol thought.

Even though it was the middle of the night, she was working at full speed. "First, there was important work done on the lines that made them more reliable, so more product could be put through. The work was done as soon as we moved out, and it was charged to the new plant. Neither the work nor the cost showed up in the material I had to work with. Mathews was hiding it. And he was hiding the cost of Canadian blocks of fish and using the cost of the Asian blocks for everything. There isn't a lot of the Canadian fish, but over a year it adds up, and since it doesn't have to travel any distance, it comes in a little cheaper."

Carol said, "In other words, there is solid evidence that it makes better sense than we knew to buy the old plant."

"It almost does." ·

"But?"

Carol wondered how much of this kind of thing Baxter had done. She said, trying it out on Annette and herself and Baxter, "I'm thinking Mathews wanted the old plant to look just efficient enough to justify a sale, should anyone bother to check, not that his fake buyer was going to check. Through his fake buyer he wanted to be able to buy the old plant as cheaply as possible. Once he had it, as a little bonus along with everything else, he'd be able to sell the improved lines for more than the value of the old lines that supposedly he'd gotten with his purchase."

"Except he didn't get the old plant." Annette had put it all together without quite knowing.

Carol said, "Annette, you've nailed it."

"Yes, but, and I know you explained this. You really didn't already know all this?" Annette giggled nervously into the phone and asked, "Is it all right to be having fun?"

"It's supposed to be fun. I'm having fun, too. So what do we need now?"

"Everything we can get about customers. Everything about suppliers. Everything about production at the old plant. And competitor pricing."

"Perfect. Garcia, the engineer, should bring production news down to the old plant at eight thirty. You get the customers and suppliers and pricing. I want to think about the brand."

"I don't have to come down to the old plant this morning. I know it runs."

"I'd like you to come, Annette. You're too important, and you'd be missed. And bring copies of the pricing you built against the offer on the old plant, along with the stuff on the line improvements and the Canadian fish, and if you want to escape having to talk about it all, some one-page summaries of everything. After that, call whoever works in finance, and anybody else useful, get them into the new plant and looking for the information about customers and suppliers. Let's pretend we're going to have all we need by the time Baxter Blume gets here. The lead Baxter Blume guy will be a friend, but even so, it'll be his baby when he gets here, and I don't want to be stepping on his toes to get this or that possibly helpful file. Also, it might be helpful to know whether the fat boys were padding their salaries."

"They gave themselves bonuses at each milestone toward completion of the new plant."

"Good. That'll give my friend Remy another stick for keeping them off our backs." Carol said that.

And then she couldn't stop herself from saying, "What about Dave Parks?"

Annette said, "Was Dave a crook, too? Is that what you're asking?"

This was one question she didn't want to ask without a lot of preparation. It certainly wasn't a question Annette should have to answer. Carol said, "We're working with him, regardless."

Annette said, "He did not take the bonuses. Do you want to know if I'm a crook, too?"

Carol didn't say a word.

Annette said, "Well, I'm not."

Since her first burials, if Carol couldn't be sure about somebody, and she needed them too much to get rid of them, she kept an eye on them and focused their work as tightly as she could. You learned that it never helped wheels go around when you asked people if they were rats, whether they were rats or not.

Annette said, "None of us liked being sold to the Germans and then the Japanese. After that happens a couple of times, you don't care as much about the company. Some people are going to say the hell with it. Dave didn't, and neither did I."

Annette sounded hurt and angry, and frankly, the last thing Carol wanted was to lose Annette, or Dave Parks. She sensed another punch coming from Annette, and she waited for it.

"Can I ask you something, Carol?"

Here it came. Carol said, "Sure."

"Are you a crook, Carol?"

Carol was relieved that Annette had asked. She hoped it would clear the air. She said, "Thank you for asking, Annette. No. I haven't always gotten it right, but, no. I'm a pretty straight businessman, like you, like Dave."

Annette said, the hurt and anger gone from her voice, "Except you and I are women. And you know, there won't be windows to the outside at the old plant, when we move the offices downstairs. There may not be electricity either, if we can't figure out where that's going."

"Let's worry about the electricity. But can we have fun without windows?"

"Yes."

"Then the hell with the windows."

Carol hung up with Annette feeling, surprisingly, that they had done all kinds of useful work, even if she wasn't sure what all the kinds were.

She called Parks to set up a midday meeting with everybody at the new plant, after they'd gone through things at the old plant.

She also told him about what else Annette had found in Mathews's separate file cabinet during the night.

He said, "Far freaking out."

Carol said, "Absolutely. And Annette is good."

"Annette is good," Parks said. "Also, you know, we won't have windows downstairs, which means we'll all smell like fish sticks."

"If that's the least of it, I want to smell like a fish stick."

Carol was feeling satisfied herself. She had her team, the heart of her organization, in place. She'd gotten extra leverage on the fat boys if she needed it, and she'd gotten a free upgrade on the lines in the plant along with the possible benefit of Canadian fish. She'd also gotten Baxter to send her people to bury the new plant and set up an offering for the old one. That she'd gotten his blessing was not a practical thing, but it mattered to her.

⋏

She hung up with Parks and went into her laptop. She set up a document with her last 1040 and a summary of her net worth. She didn't dwell on how pitiful the Baxters of the world would find her net. She didn't dwell on what the line workers would think. She didn't dwell on how much of it she'd have to risk to open the wallets of the once and future employees of Elizabeth's Fish and the citizens of Elizabeth Island. She wanted everybody who invested to be able to know that she was putting herself at serious risk.

⋏

She got in the car and drove down to the harbor.

It was four o'clock in the morning. The rain was done. She was not the least bit tired, and it was not the old plant she wanted to see. She was feeling as if anything could happen and all of it would be good, and she went to the other side of the harbor, to where Easy Parsons's boat was tied up.

The tide must have been higher, and she came along the common pier and between the buildings to face the superstructure of his boat. His bright deck lights weren't on, and she turned off her own headlights. There were security lights on the pier, but she was parked in shadow.

She got out of the car and walked to the edge of the pier and looked into the working deck. It was a big boat, but it wouldn't be big out of sight of land. It didn't look like Easy was around. She could have gone on board, but in the steps it had taken her to walk from her car, all her confidence had evaporated. She didn't know if she was more shy about going on his boat when he wasn't there or when he was. She went back to her car and closed the door and sat for a minute. She took off the jacket to her suit and folded it on the seat beside her and closed her eyes.

She heard the gulls and knew she had been sleeping. It was light but not yet bright.

Her first thought was that she had her own company, and for an instant she didn't believe it and was frightened and pissed off and missing her dad, and then just as quick it was all real and everything was terrific.

On the hood of the car was a red and white canister of Quaker Oats.

Easy sat on a rubber tub beside her window. He wore jeans and the kind of worked-in chambray shirt that the shark at the town meeting last night would never own. His arms reached over his knees. He was studying his boat and he looked happy.

She tried to put down her window, but the car wasn't running. She started the car, and Easy waved as if she were leaving. Carol laughed.

She put down the window and turned off the car, and behind him the pier ran out a hundred yards lined with cold-storage sheds and small, shuttered seafood outfits.

She smiled and said, "What's with the oatmeal?"

From a paper bag, he took a banana and an apple and a green paper carton of strawberries and put them on the hood beside the oats.

There out her windshield, everything looked as brightly pretty and surprising as she could imagine. She guessed he'd heard she wanted oatmeal and fruit at St. Peter's Breakfast. She said, "Small world."

"When we go out on my boat, you won't think small world."

She wasn't sure if he was inviting her onto his boat right now, but she realized that if she left the car here, people would see it and think she'd spent the night on Easy's boat. She wasn't sure whether or not she wanted anyone to think that, though she had come all the way down here.

Easy said, "You kissed me last night."

That sounded like another invitation. She wanted to kiss him again. That was why she'd come down here. But she wasn't ready. She said, as if it were a conversation she had all the time, "I haven't brushed my teeth."

He let her off the hook. "Then let's walk to breakfast at St. Pete's," he said.

She got out of the car and closed her door, and he leaned back in her window and, like he'd spent his whole life knowing to do it, got her jacket.

Water Line

He didn't jump up and down, didn't want to scare her off, but Easy had himself a date.

St. Peter was so interested in doing Carol the giant favor of making oatmeal and cutting up fruit and checking with Carol that he was getting it right, that there wasn't time for Carol and Easy to talk. Next came the old-timers who crawled in every morning to see if anybody'd died, and they figured out Carol was the one who had spoken at Town Hall the night before. Which made it a responsibility they tell her what it had been like in their day, when you could walk across the harbor on fishing boats. And that was true, but again no conversation between Easy and Carol. Still, it was sweet to see her relax into being accepted in this harbor breakfast dive. Had to be nicer for her than going from one town to the next, year after year, without ever belonging. Today she belonged.

As they walked on down to the old plant, Easy thought about holding her hand and didn't. He didn't want to distract her if she was getting into her business frame of mind. Either that or he was afraid.

He wondered if she was nervous around him. She had kissed him. For him, it had been a while since he'd touched a woman, and since Mississippi, since Angie died, Carol was the first woman he'd wanted to care about. Last night he was all there for kissing her. This morning, after being so proud about getting a date with a nice-looking woman, he was afraid to hold her hand, and he figured if he got past that, he would probably make both of them unhappy. He wanted to run home to the boat.

As the two of them approached the plant, it wasn't hard to pick up that they were the center of attention for Parks and Buddy and Annette Novato and Anna Rose, which killed what was left of the date thing for Easy. Ben Garcia was there, too, and Easy didn't know him more than to nod hello, but he was the engineer for the old plant, and looked like he was fifteen.

Carol got rid of the stares by introducing herself to Garcia and asking if he knew the plant well enough to run it.

Easy, freed from attention, settled in to watch Carol do her stuff.

Garcia said, "I know this plant like my pocket," an answer that made Carol laugh. Garcia was up from El Salvador, and had an accent, but so did a lot of Elizabeth Island, and Garcia smiled like he had just come up with his line.

Carol studied him, and Garcia stood straight and looked back at her. He looked respectful and also like he could hold his own. Carol said, "How long would it take to get it running?"

"We have cooking oil and batter. We have boxes for shipping at dropdown. It is only waiting."

"Can you keep it running?"

Everybody else was concentrated on following along, but Easy was admiring how sharp Carol was, how she was finding out what she needed to know about the plant and Garcia both. A small thing, but it spoke to Easy about how capable Carol was. Easy liked capable.

Garcia, matter-of-fact but on the nose, said, "It is simple. Like the old Detroit cars: iron, manual transmission, carburetor. Turn it on, let it go. Change the oil every thousand miles. And I still can work as foreman." Easy could have used Ben Garcia on the boat, and he figured Carol had already come to the same conclusion about Garcia and her plant.

She said, "Would you turn on part of a line so that Mr. Taormina can see something work?"

Garcia started for the door with his ball of keys and had the lights on in seconds and then, in another minute, a belt going at the head of the first line.

Easy had not been in the plant for years, but you couldn't miss that work had been done. Buddy was noticing the same thing. The lines looked like they'd had major upgrading.

Easy said, "Ben, the lines look shinier."

Garcia looked a little less head-on, at first, but then stood into it. He said, "Mr. Mathews ordered as soon as everybody moved up to the new plant. He paid me overtime to be here and see it all went in good, asked me not to talk about it because it was separate from the company, for selling this plant. The work was good and the plant was already left behind, so I didn't feel it was wrong. Also they brought one truck and the men in at night and out by the end of the next night. I don't know about all that, but I know machinery, and for these lines, it was a little quicker, also more reliable, besides prettier; a good thing, no question. For me, too, and my family, the overtime money helped. I wouldn't be saying anything now because I promised, except he doesn't own the plant anymore."

Buddy and his mother were surprised like Easy, but Carol and Parks and Annette Novato were not.

Carol said, "It's fine, Ben, a good thing." To Buddy and Anna Rose, she said, "We found out about it in the private file cabinet Mathews kept. One more of his games, but it works for us; it gives us some extra value and a better chance keeping up with the big processing outfits."

Buddy said, "That jerk."

Anna Rose said, "I am not going to listen to you speak like that."

Easy was already back to watching Carol. She said, "Go ahead, Ben."

Garcia said, "It all works pretty much the same. I can light the ovens over here, after the basting. You would see flames if you want."

Carol said, "Buddy?"

Buddy said, "No, that's all right."

Garcia said, "You want to walk all of it?"

Carol looked to Buddy, who said, "I knew it would run if it was still here. I just wanted to be sure those jerks hadn't gutted the place. I guess, yeah, great if they fixed it up some. I lumped for the water line as a kid in summer. Remember, Ma? And Maria was with the cutters until Dad found out. Hey, Ben. How about that? Do you know anything about the water line?"

Garcia headed for the dock wall.

Easy remembered the water lines from all the times when he was a kid and had fed them out of his father's hold. He had no idea how long since they were used, but he watched Carol check everything out, and he thought that, given a day, she could probably get the whole plant up and running again by herself.

Easy liked the plant. It reminded him of his boat—not pretty but useful. The belt at the head of the first line echoed like gravel.

The ceiling had blackened above the fluorescents. The walls were yellowed stucco, hung with watermark. The floor was concrete gone iron with rust and stained by dry pools of sickly green. The lines hunched up and down through the room. Actually, the rust on the floor could be blood from all the thumbs lost to shattered flywheels.

Carol interrupted Easy's musing. She said, "All the plants I shut down had old machinery held together with not much more than hope and chewing gum. Sometimes, when the people were emptied out, I cared for the dead machinery more than a real factory, because it had been loved all the way to the end."

That was how Easy had felt, and why he couldn't bear his own empty house without Angie and the baby they'd made ready for. It was how he imagined the bones of his father's boat off the Georges.

Parks said, "Carol. I don't think that's the note we want to strike just now."

Carol laughed with everybody else, but Easy thought she was beautiful for what she had said. Besides which he thought there was a good chance she'd find his boat beautiful. He went ahead and said that, courageous and happy both. "Wait until you get a good look at my boat."

More laughing, from everybody, but he thought Carol gave him an extra nod.

She said, "Now. Where were we?"

Annette Novato pointed off to one wall where there was a warren of alcoves with partitions that didn't come close to reaching the ceiling. Then Carol, pointing at one alcove that jutted into the floor, said, "Corner office."

Parks pointed at a stain on the floor and said, "We had business from McDonald's and lost it, and we won't get them back with the way the place looks. But the inspections come up clean, so it's mostly cosmetics." Easy had expected a golden oldie on floor stains, but he knew Parks well enough around town to have seen a smart guy underneath the songs. Parks, along with the kidding, kept things in focus. Another good guy to have around. Carol was hiring all the best crew.

There was a rolling rumble from across the width of the building, and a bright slice of sunlight shot in through the wall. The rumble continued as Garcia pushed the dock doors open wider, and the day poured into the cave of the plant.

Buddy said, "It's ready for business, Ma."

"Of course it's ready," Anna Rose said. "I told you it was ready."

Garcia was folding blue plastic tarp off of the simple series of belts and countertops that had been stacked in sections along the open wall.

Buddy said to Carol, "They called it the water line because it was next to the water and brought in the fish fresh from the boats. Used to be a couple of lines."

Garcia said, "I never saw it run, but I have set it up before to know. It is nothing to work. Just people cut the fish."

"Look, Ma. The saws. Remember when Maria was cutting the heads off whiting and Dad found out?"

Annette Novato said something about still not seeing the missing electricity.

Anna Rose led everybody out onto the dock, saying, "Why do you remember those things, Ignacio? Let Carol see what a beautiful city we have."

Easy looked. It was a beautiful city, if you could call it a city. The late lobster and day boats were still clustered at the head of the inner harbor, dirty reds and yellows and blues, their guys dragging bait barrels from the pickups. Just behind them was the back of the hardware and lumberyard and the back of the appliance place with the grandson still holding out against the Sears off the island. The back of the St. Peter's club was there where Main Street came down to the harbor road, and at the other end of things were the windows of the Peg Leg, where the Lions and Rotary and all the others held their meetings until the bottom of the summer crowd came to eat either the dregs of local catch or frozen from God knew where. Most of the buildings up the hill were still the stone and brick they'd always been, and they had a worn importance with being solid and with having been there years, and the edging of their rooftops was greened copper. As the hill rounded side to side higher up, there were the wood buildings, the houses with some of the colors still true and with pointy roofs, lonely looking houses from up close but postcard pretty from here. Away to the right, you could see the two blue steeples of the Portuguese church, and from here on the plant dock, which Easy had never realized, you could actually see the Our Lady between the steeples holding her boat. You couldn't see the big Italian Catholic church, going the other way to the Italian end of town, but there were a couple more wooden steeples tucked in, Yankee steeples, his own among them for as long as there was anyone to drag him, and the trees were becoming green up there. His city. It was hurting, and had been hurting for a while, but you didn't see that. You saw, Easy saw, and he believed Carol would see, how beautiful it was. He was glad Anna Rose had said something.

Anna Rose said, "Is that your car, Easy? Do you have a new car?"

All of them lined along the dock looking across the harbor at Carol's car beyond Easy's boat.

"Out-of-state plates," Buddy said.

Carol said, "It's my car." Said it just like that and no more. Straightened up some, maybe took a deep breath that only Easy saw because he was looking for it. She stared across at her car and let the quiet be the quiet. She was a strong woman, first to last. Easy didn't care what people thought about him, but he didn't want anybody assuming things about Carol. Now was a time when Easy wanted to put an arm around her, which would have been stupid and would also have taken courage he could only ever dream of. What he did, he looked away out at the harbor, pretending to see any sort of something fishermanly, pure chickenshit.

Anna Rose said, "It is Carol's car, Ignacio. Mind your business."

Carol stood between Buddy and Garcia and said, "It is a beautiful town." Then she turned to Buddy and said, "And you believe the plant can work?"

So much for the car. Good going, Carol. Only, now, Easy wondered if she was starting to think, like he was, what it would be like if they had spent the night together.

Buddy said, "I'm in, Carol. You'll be seeing me and my fish off your dock here as soon as you're ready."

Good to have Buddy say that. Easy said, "Me, too."

Anna Rose said, "Carol. Maybe you didn't see this." She pulled a rolled section of newspaper out of her clothes. "The *Boston Globe*. Front page. From the meeting right here in Elizabeth. The agency will tell the judge she should not enforce the amendment. Even the environmentalists agree. And now fishermen are environmentalists, too, Carol. We are helping the fish to come back. So if Ignacio thinks he has to know the plant is working, Carol, you can know that Ignacio and Ezekiel will be able to bring you fish. Don't worry about that."

Buddy said, "Thank you, Ma, for that instruction."

Garcia, still looking across at the car, said to Carol, "You tune?"

Easy said, "Forget the car, Garcia." He didn't say it loud, because Garcia wasn't sniggering, but enough about the damn car.

Carol nodded at Garcia and said, "Once upon a time," and both of them nodded.

Then Carol gave Easy a cool-it tilt of the head. He took a breath and cooled it.

Parks said, "So, Carol."

Parks was a smart guy and a guy who kept an eye out. He'd probably picked up on all of it: Easy saying what he hadn't had to say to Garcia, and Carol's tilt.

But Parks was going somewhere else. He said, "Somebody has to ask it out loud, Carol. You're an undertaker. You bury places. Can you run this place?"

If somebody besides Parks had asked that, Easy might have said something, but Parks looked like he knew what he was doing, and Carol had given the cool-it tilt, and really she looked fine with the question.

She said, "The fact is, I don't think I can run it."

Carol said that and looked out over the harbor coming blue under the early sun. Everybody was quiet, including Easy, who was way out of his league here. Carol must have practiced at quiet. She turned, looked up at the brick and the stone and green copper roof trim toward Town Hall and the steeples. No argument it was a beat-up town, but nobody'd deny it was beautiful.

Just when everybody was getting used to the quiet, Carol came back on.

She said again, this time with muscle, "I don't think I can run it."

Then she said, "I am running it."

That sank in, and she said, "We'll have a company in a matter of days, and this plant will be up in a matter of weeks. For now, Ben, you get oriented inside, figure out who you need and clear that with Dave. We'll have to clean and paint. Give some thought to that."

Had she worked that out with Parks? Easy didn't think so. Maybe Parks had just wanted her to step up. But Easy would have bet Carol was waiting for the right chance to step up. Leaving him, a fisherman, feeling landlocked. He'd better be ready to step up himself.

But what was really on Easy's mind was how pretty Carol was and that her car was right there across the harbor by his boat, as if . . . he wasn't sure as if what. He wanted to hold her first.

Going to the Kitchens

As everybody came out of the dim of the plant, somebody got Carol's arm from behind to hold her back, and at first she thought it would be Easy. She smiled because she was happily worried that Easy was going to collect his kiss right now, for God sake.

It was Anna Rose. "Some of us, especially our Wives of the Sea, talk to one another about the things you said last night, our history and our harbor. Others don't want to talk; they want to forget and be done. It was difficult for all of us, everybody, having a stranger stand up and put her nose into other people's families and how we live and who has died. But you said it like you were in church. Everybody heard that, and when they heard it, they were surprised. Me and the Wives of the Sea and also the others; you made us see our dead and remember like the first time. No one liked it, but it was what we needed."

When she'd finished, Anna Rose clamped her short arms around Carol and squeezed. Her head came to Carol's chin. Carol was not used to hugs. It had only been her and her father in their house, and what hugging there was had been as awkward as it was rare. She was glad Anna Rose had said what she'd said, but Carol was a business-man in the middle of something, and Anna Rose did not give a quick hug, and Carol's arms were trapped. The hug went on until finally Carol laid her head down on top of Anna Rose's head.

Anna Rose hugged a moment more, then pulled away and looked at Carol as if they had become people who had known each other forever. For some reason, it came to Carol that Baxter would doubt a hug if it ever happened. Baxter didn't deal one on one with many Anna Roses, and if he did they weren't going to think of hugging him. Carol decided that she'd liked her hug, and she put Baxter away.

"Now," Anna Rose said. "Business." And she led Carol in a march to Annette's car, where Annette had the detailed justifi-cations and was handing out copies of a one-page summary. She mentioned to Carol again that the plant was using electricity she couldn't account for, and Carol cared about anything on Annette's mind, but the electric bills would have to wait.

Out from behind the bulk of the plant, the sun came up on the old, idled cold-storage building, peeled and half repainted in industrial greens and blues and the fading black of abandoned signage.

Carol took a copy of the summary and pretended to study it. It was brief and it looked doable. All Carol had to do was close. She didn't care how Baxter closed; she wasn't Baxter.

The price on the old Elizabeth's Fish plant was next to noth-ing. Even Ben Garcia knew that.

It was also a ton.

Or was it?

Was it a ton to Anna Rose?

Was it really a ton to Elizabeth Island?

Carol wanted to say, "We can do it."

She glanced at Easy as if he might have a suggestion. He was watching her, probably to see how she'd handle things.

What she said, with calculated hesitance, was "We can go to the banks," and she knew that if Baxter were here he would be grinning like the used car salesman he was. This was how he did it.

She said, "Frankly, I doubt we can raise this much among ourselves and in town. But with what we can raise, and with the competitive pricing we can show because of our fresh fish business and the office rentals and the refurbished lines, we might be able to find a banker." She spun it out in quasi-business vernacular to disguise the manipulation.

She could all but hear Baxter whispering, "Yes."

She said, "This is a whole lot more than we're likely to come close to raising. I wish we could, and you know better than I do, but Elizabeth's not a big town or an especially wealthy town. We may find fewer investors than we hope. On the other hand, we might find more than one banker and muster some pushback on the rates. I'm willing to put in half of my net worth to start the ball rolling, and work at least a couple of years on subsistence salary with some performance options, but I don't have deep enough pockets myself. I hate to do it, but it looks like banks are the only option."

She paused. She glanced at Easy. She hoped he would understand. After all, she'd just promised a lot of her own money. She took a breath to go on, and in her head, Baxter told her, "Don't say another word."

Carol didn't say another word. She looked down at her summary like everybody else. She wanted the plant, and she didn't want bankers. She didn't want to pay the rates they'd insist on. She didn't want to give up the control they'd insist she give up. She didn't want anybody saying she couldn't go right to the edge, and this plant was going to be on the edge for a while before suppliers and customers developed any confidence. Even in her dreams, this would never be any kind of growth engine, and as long as it was on the edge, it wouldn't want to pay a penny of its cash flow on debt. If they worked their way back from the edge, they'd want a credit line, and they'd use it, but right now, please, she didn't want bankers.

She looked at her plant and she walked away from everybody. She could almost hear Baxter laughing.

Anna Rose said, "This is not so much money." She said it loudly, after Carol, though Carol had not walked very far. The volume was for anyone who thought Elizabeth couldn't afford its fish plant.

It was working. Carol was closing, and now she felt guilty about it, about Anna Rose. Baxter would feel no guilt. He'd say, "Don't be ridiculous."

Carol glanced at Easy, who kept his head down over his summary. She told herself that this company was a good thing. It was a good thing, and she was doing what she could to make it happen.

Parks said, "It's a fair price. The plant can justify it. I have no problem trying to sell shares in this."

Carol started to turn around to enter the conversation, and Baxter said, "For Christ sake do not turn around yet."

Ben Garcia, bless his heart, the least likely guy in the circle, the furthest outside outsider, said, "I will invest in this plant, and I know more people who will invest."

Baxter said, "If I didn't know better, I'd say you planted him."

"I'm in," Buddy Taormina said.

"What do we need bankers for this?" Anna Rose said. "This is not so much we need bankers. I thought we decided no bankers."

Carol turned around.

Anna Rose said, "Our town is not so poor. For this much, it is not poor at all."

Parks said, "I think she's probably right. We can get this."

"It is no probably," Anna Rose said. "What do bankers want with our building here? If they lend to us, they want us to fail so they can have the land and wait for condominiums at the next zoning."

Carol started to speak, and Baxter said, "Shut up."

Anna Rose said, "We can raise this much money in two, three days. We need more for emergencies, we can raise that. We better raise that. I am putting in half of what I have, and it is not so little. Everybody else, most of them, we don't ask so much to risk, and we don't have to ask so much. And some can give plenty and never notice. Two, three days."

Easy was staring at Carol. He said, "You ought to be selling used cars, Carol."

She made herself look him in the eye, but her heart was going oh-gee-whiz.

He said, "I hope you sell fish as good as you sell this run-down factory nobody wants."

He didn't say it as hard as it sounded. He was almost teasing, she thought.

Baxter said, "Tell this deltabilly to ante up and go trawl."

Carol said, "I'm putting my own money where my mouth is," and wished she didn't sound defensive.

He shrugged and said, "It's good, Carol." He smiled, and she felt relieved.

Then she got hold of herself and turned mercilessly to Anna Rose. Anna Rose dove in. "Easy Parsons can give plenty. He owns that boat outright, and he is a high liner. I hate to say it—I am from generations of fishermen, and Ignacio is as good a fisherman as any of them—but Easy brings in more fish quicker than any captain from New Bedford to Portland. Easy is going to give us one hundred thousand dollars, and then he is going to make us listen to him. Ignacio owns two boats, but not both outright, and he has a family, so maybe he only gives a hundred thousand also."

Garcia said, "I have family here and much family in El Salvador, and I will give two thousand."

Parks said, "This is why I haven't slept," and he turned away from the group the way Carol had done.

But Carol didn't think Parks was turning away to manipulate anybody. She expected he was deciding whether to really jump in. He faced the large, abandoned cold-storage building that belonged to the plant but was outside the fence. If Parks, who knew more than anyone else, pulled his rip cord, it was over. All of them knew that, and Carol knew she would not get another chance like this.

He turned back around and said, "I can commit two hundred and fifty thousand dollars. We're core investors, and we're at the heart of operations. If we're going to sell it, we better own it."

Carol couldn't laugh when Parks had just kicked in a nervous quarter of a million dollars, but she was glad.

When Easy held up two fingers, she didn't understand until Parks said, "What's that, big guy?"

"Two hundred thousand dollars," Anna Rose said. "He will give two hundred thousand, but now he is not talking because I said he would talk too much. Good. You sound best not talking, Ezekiel."

Buddy said, "I can go a hundred and a half, but I'd rather start at a hundred."

Carol said, "I can do eight hundred thousand."

"I will put in three hundred thousand," Anna Rose said.

"Ma."

"Mind your own business. You don't know what I have."

Annette said, "I have twelve thousand dollars."

Carol said, "Take a day to think about that. I want you on the team regardless. You, too, Ben."

Annette said, "I've thought about it. If we get close and need extra, I can invest another six thousand."

"Fair enough."

"And now," Anna Rose said, "we all together come to the kitchens."

Carol laughed and said, "Yes. To the kitchens, Anna Rose."

Anna Rose said, "I will make meetings for tonight and for tomorrow night, maybe the night after that."

Garcia said, "I will help with my own people."

Carol said, "Okay, but you have to come everywhere else, too, Ben. You answer the questions about whether and how the plant runs. I'd be surprised if there weren't questions."

Then she said to Parks, "What about the golfers and the Chamber, those people?"

Parks said, "My territory. I'll put that kitchen together. Some of them will be Mathews's pals, but I think they may want in regardless. Buddy, you and Easy need to set something up for the harbor guys your mother doesn't reach."

"Yes, but also," Anna Rose said, "we need Ignacio and Ezekiel to come with us to all the kitchens so that people know we have the fresh fish."

Baxter whispered, "Do not be in a room asking for money while that guy flirts with you."

Carol told Baxter it was his turn to shut up, and the next thing out of her mouth was "Do we want Easy in the kitchens with us?"

Which she meant to sound like she was teasing him, but it sounded like Baxter. She looked at Easy and laughed so he'd know it was teasing, and even the laugh came out wrong.

Buddy joined in the laughter and pushed at Easy as if they were teenagers.

Easy looked away from Carol as if he were surprised and then right away looked back and grinned as if he couldn't care less.

Carol blushed with shame. She'd said something mean. And worse, it was true—she didn't want Easy in the kitchens disrupting her pitch for the money they needed to go forward.

"No," Anna Rose said. "We need Easy. He is the best fisherman in our harbor and everyone will want to see he is with you. If only we could keep him from talking—you are right about that."

Carol said, "Easy, forgive me. I want you in every room where we sell this business."

She hoped he would say something that forgave her. He left her alone.

She said, "I'm sorry. I am sorry. I wish I hadn't sounded mean."

She didn't care what everyone else was thinking. And then she had to move on.

She told everyone as quickly as she could about two guys arriving late in the day from Baxter Blume to sell off the new plant and set up the stock offering for the old plant. She arranged to meet Parks at the new plant in half an hour to talk to the women on the line there. She told everybody to keep in touch with one another and with her.

She said loudly, a battle cry, "To the kitchens."

Parks picked it right up. "To the kitchens."

They, all of them but Easy and Carol, went to their cars calling, "To the kitchens."

Carol walked next to Easy back along the narrow lane of sheds and the lobster building. Easy went in his lunging stride as if she were not there. He wore a green and blue plaid shirt over a black T-shirt, and he had on jeans and work boots, and Carol thought he belonged in this lane. He swung his boots; he swung the long bounce of his gait and the lengths of his arms.

Carol had a meeting in less than half an hour, and she walked fast the way she did. She was eager for her meeting, and yet this lane of decayed industrial waterfront was as gorgeous to her as the inside of the factory. Potholes held water from last night's rain, and that water held the blue of the sky in oily iridescence.

She said, "Wait."

He didn't stop, and she said, "Please."

She went half a dozen steps over to a corrugated wall that had been painted and faded to a surgical green only seven or eight feet up its twenty-foot height. The rest of the wall was battleship gray with chalk mottlings of bird splatter and brown runs of rust. She stood against the wall in her dark blue suit, and she spread her arms.

Easy looked at her, but she could not tell if he saw her. She was afraid that if he didn't see her, no one who mattered would ever see her again. Dominic had seen her. She stayed where she was, as she was. She was a beauty in that lane, she had to be, and she closed her eyes. She heard his boots.

He put a callused finger on her lips. This was what Easy Parsons felt like. Before she could open her eyes, he kissed her. She didn't even think to put her arms around him before he stopped and said, "You have a meeting at the new plant." He didn't laugh at that. She kissed him back, and he said, "Sooner or later," and took her hand, and they walked around the rest of the harbor like that, holding hands.

Carol felt sick in her stomach because she knew how much effort and time it would take to make her company go. She didn't mind that. She wanted her company. But she wanted Easy, too.

From Now On

As soon as she connected with Parks at the new plant, Carol put on a hair bag and a smock and shoe covers, and brought all the office staff down onto the floor. Annette was still confused about electricity usage in the old plant, and Carol said, "Okay. Let's get on it," and put it out of her mind.

She knew she'd want to stand on something, but she hadn't planned that out. She looked around at the women who were the regular plant laborers. She looked as many in the eye as she could, and she nodded and smiled without pretending to be friends. She wanted to appear as if she were in charge and as if it didn't matter what they thought of her. She had been on plant floors before this one, but this time was different.

She stood up straight and let the women look into her, and she hoped they could see she understood what plant work meant. She hoped they could see she was honest and was capable of running a company. She hoped they could see she was nervous but that she was steady despite being nervous.

She stood among them until all of the office staff, including Parks and Annette, was down and had mingled. In her father's plants, and in almost all the places she'd shut down, the people in the offices were apart, upstairs mostly, so the upstairs was mostly the enemy. Her father called it "the upstairs" and hated and worshiped it.

In the working women's faces here today, Carol saw envy, judgment, and curiosity, eagerness for a deal, and readiness to do work. She saw kindness and anxiousness and readiness to laugh. She saw assertion and reticence. She saw plain women and strong women and women who had been pretty and pretty girls who were tough. She saw a lot of reluctance to hope.

She looked down at a concrete floor that was so new the gray floor paint still had its gloss. She saw her feet massive in the shoe covers. She had great green hooves.

There had been a face that had looked able to laugh, and Carol tried to remember which one.

She looked up and searched the faces again and found that face, and she engaged those eyes.

Then she lifted one foot.

She looked at her raised foot, the giant hoof, and looked again at the eyes that might laugh. She imagined Baxter on the floor, which would have been a first for him and not a happy one.

She looked at her hoof again, and stood down on it, and then hopped, da-dum, da-dum, from hoof to hoof. She hopped like a kid pretending to ride a horse. She made just the gesture of her hands holding the reins.

It took no more than an instant. But everyone saw.

It was an instant that seemed an hour and made firing people seem a walk in the park.

And she heard Baxter's voice in her head say, "What the hell are you doing?"

The woman made a low chuckle.

Carol heard that and made one more da-dum, da-dum, with her hands pulling on the reins now and her eyes on her horse and leaning back to stop.

The chuckle became a laugh.

Then Carol looked up at the woman who was laughing and laughed herself. They looked at each other and it was funny and they laughed out loud, and now she could look around at all of the other faces again, and they laughed. They laughed at Carol and they laughed with her. They laughed wondering what was going on, but they laughed.

She stood in her blue suit and her smock and her hair bag and her shoe covers, full of news, and Baxter said, "All right. Screw me."

She let go of her horse and relaxed from the laughter and let everyone else relax.

She walked toward the first of the lines, and the women let her through, and she said to no one in particular, "Can I stand here on a part of the line?"

She was at a black belt on rollers and its stainless sheathing. She put her hands on the edge and looked around. "Will I break the belt?"

Somebody pushed through to spread a clean cloth over the edge and the belt. One of the Asian women.

Another woman said, "I'll get a stepladder."

Carol said, "I'm okay," and she reached under her smock and hitched her pants and swung a knee up. She could still climb onto something she wanted to climb onto.

She didn't worry about what she looked like. She was who she was, and this was what she wanted to do and how she wanted to do it, and she didn't give a shit about Baxter.

There were other hands on her, steadying her, some actually pushing to help her up.

She said, "Thank you," without looking back. She put her weight on her own hands and got one foot beneath her and then the other. She gathered her balance, as much on the edging as she could be, and she stood.

She turned around to face them all, and the Asian woman who had brought the cloth looked up at her and said, "Phwoo," with a gasp of breath as if she had had to climb up herself.

There was enough quiet that the "Phwoo" sounded out.

Carol said, "Phwoo," and there was another general laugh.

Then she said, "Take a look around," and she looked around herself at the fat boys' new and too-shiny plant.

The walls were as glossy as the floor. Almost everything else but the belts, and there was a lot of everything else, was stainless. There was some signage, and some OSHA cautions in small red squares. There were a few yellow components beneath what must have been the ovens. There were lines of orange hosing. There were other stairs and there were gates and double doors for equipment. There were tracks to and from the freezers. There was a small, isolated line in its own alcove that she knew was for experimental products, though she was sure that the fat boys had never done, or imagined doing, any experiments. Overhead, weaving under and through brand-new iron roof trusses, painted a nice Rust-Oleum orange, were the tin and stainless ducts and vents and fans.

It was the opposite of the old plant. It was all whitewalls and chrome next to her bent Mustang. She liked her Mustang and she liked her old plant.

The people before her were quiet.

She said, "It's a pretty place." It was quiet, and she said, "You won't work again in a place as pretty as this." Now the quiet was listening in a different way. She said, "From here on out, it gets ugly." Nobody was about to laugh now, and she didn't smile. She said it and let it sit. All of the faces listened, and she listened with them. She looked once more around the fat boys' meal ticket, and she heard a few feet shuffle in restlessness. She said, "From now on." The shuffling stopped, and she said, "From now on, we're going to be working in the old plant."

Carol took a deep breath. She hadn't just said something good—and she knew she had—she had said what she had wanted to say at burial after burial for all those years.

人

She thought she was fine by the time she got upstairs. She tried to lead Annette and three executive assistants back to the copy room on the executive floor, where they had been working since early that morning. But Annette stopped her, said "Thank you," and held out her hand to shake, and then the other three said "Thank you" and shook her hand, and Carol teared up. She put an arm around Annette's shoulders.

She let go of Annette and said, "Okay," loudly, and everybody laughed. Then they went on and sorted piles and handed paper back and forth and ran copies of the takeaway material for suppliers and customers and anybody else who might be helpful. Aside from the five of them, the floor was empty.

It was mind-numbing work, but everything was falling into place as if it had all been waiting for her. She had only arrived the day before yesterday. She needed to ask Baxter how worried she ought to be. This was more of a roll than she'd ever been on in her life, and it was exhilarating, and she couldn't believe she deserved it.

She wondered if her father would be proud. He would read the old plant. He would register the exploded asphalt around it and the battered loading dock. He would see deferred maintenance—abandoned maintenance it looked like. He would remember their old neighborhood and see the deferred maintenance in those plants spreading like a virus before he died. It would have reached his bench if he'd lived. He might say, "You're a CEO, Carol," and try to let her know he was impressed, but he would understand she was the CEO of a brick trying to float.

From down the hall came Remy's voice shouting, "Hey, Carol," and she kicked into that gear. She was glad she'd get to see Remy as a friend, and she also wondered what kind of a deal she could get from him for all the office hardware on this floor. She knew she couldn't afford brand new, but suddenly she wanted brand-new copiers, and brand-new desks; she even wanted new carpet.

Whoever Remy had brought with him said, "Where's the Beast?"

"Where *is* the Beast?" Remy said.

Neither of them said it unkindly, and Carol almost called out, "I'm here."

She stopped herself from that, and Annette and the three assistants kept at their work in the copy room, watching Carol for a signal.

"You boys looking for Ms. MacLean?" It was Easy, talking slowly and firmly, with the kind of authority she imagined he had on his boat. "Around here, we call her Beauty. Try calling that. Call Beauty, see if it don't get you an answer. Like this—try, 'You here, Beauty?'" And just like that, Easy Parsons had chased away the Beast.

and wedding photography and secondhand clothing stores, also closed. Then a couple of small restaurants—Mexican?—that didn't seem to have many customers yet, though Carol's sense was that people here would eat early. The lower end of Main Street was the Italian side of town, and there was a sporting goods store with an Italian name she'd seen on the walls in Town Hall and a tiny cappuccino place and an Italian pizza place. The sports shop and the cappuccino place were closed, but the pizza place was open, and nobody was in there either. Carol realized that she had been the only person on the street all the way down.

Then she saw the crowd ahead, at the very bottom of the street. It looked like everyone who otherwise would have been on the street or in the restaurants, or anywhere else in Elizabeth, had gathered.

But even after seeing the sign for the St. Peter's Club, Carol couldn't make sense of it. She wondered if there had been a terrible accident. She couldn't help but wonder if that would affect the meeting and the fund-raising.

Somebody said, "Here she is," and the crowd turned as one to look at her.

And then there was Easy taking her hand and leading her through to the door of the club. People said, "Hi." They said, "Thank you" and "I was at Town Hall" and "We put from our savings into the checking" and "We brought the checkbook" and "You better believe it." And Carol smiled in a way she imagined a CEO ought to smile at a moment like this, but all she could feel was her hand in Easy's hand and his patient force bringing her through.

They would have let her through anyway, but Easy made it easy, and even so it was a crowd, and even so she held his hand tighter than she needed to. People patted her timidly and solidly on her shoulders. At the very first she avoided eye contact, and then looked into every eye she passed, and that made people happy. It made her happy. She remembered to smile. It wasn't that giant a crowd and didn't take all that long to get through, and still it seemed long. A hand patted her ass, more of a grab actually, and she turned around and laughed at a drunk as a couple other guys collared him.

When they got in the door, the crowd was still thick, all the way up the stairs. Easy looked back at her to see how she was doing and to make a pleased face that said, "How-do-you-like-this-it's-all-your-fault."

In the club's big meeting room, the crowd was still thin but fast getting thicker. Anna Rose and Annette and Ben Garcia were behind a card table facing people and handing out pens and taking checks. Parks stood behind them, and when he saw Carol, he spread his arms and looked at her as if he was baffled and there was nothing anyone could do.

Anna Rose was too busy to look up and said loudly to a hand writing a check in front of her, "Every check is a good amount and already we have some very good amounts and a few big ones."

The woman in front of Anna Rose put down the pen and looked up at Carol and smiled and nodded like Carol should know everything was going to be fine now, and another man took that woman's place and looked at Carol the same way and said, "You bet," and Anna Rose said, "Elizabeth Island's Best."

Easy leaned his forehead against the side of her temple. The crowd was thicker around them again, and before she could turn to him, he whispered into her ear, "I've got men coming on board. Will you have dinner with me when we get back? Isn't that how I ask for a date?" He was already backing away, and she shrugged like she couldn't care less, and he laughed and was off, and she put her hand up to hold his breath in her ear.

Toothfish

In two weeks, Carol had a company called Elizabeth Island's Best. They weren't running yet, but they weren't far from it. Easy had gone into Boston to off-load his catch at that auction and had gone right back out again, and back to Boston, and had called to say he would be in late last night.

Ben Garcia made space for more alcove offices around the whole perimeter of the plant floor except along the harbor wall where the water line set up. Walking down the hall to talk to someone now would mean walking around or through the plant floor, which Carol thought was great. Let the line workers see management up close day to day. Let management get face-to-face with who turned out the product and how. It was corny, and Baxter wouldn't do it, and of course her father always said that management was "the upstairs," but Carol wanted to be around the life of a plant floor.

Office windows looked onto the floor. There was sound-proofing, and the alcoves were capped, but nobody got paneling.

The build-in went fast, and it turned out that a good deal of what they needed for office equipment was still in the old offices upstairs. Carol wasn't surprised the fat boys had made side money on the new equipment in their new offices, and if they had gotten the plant, they could have sold the old office equipment along with everything else before flipping the property. As it was, with that old equipment and what Carol wheedled out of Remy, the new offices in the old plant had everything they needed, except, as Annette kept pointing out, the missing electricity.

The upstairs office space itself wasn't in bad shape, and it looked over the harbor. Carol rented it to two small law firms and a title company. She had their spaces white-boxed, their entrance polished, and a bit of parking resurfaced for them.

The whole thing, offices upstairs and downstairs, cleaning and painting the plant interior, laying in a stock of frozen pollock and cod on top of what she'd gotten at cost from Remy—none of it was unduly expensive. A significant plus was the refurbishment of the lines that Mathews had paid for.

Despite the economies, the company's cash reserves were all but gone.

You had reserves for when you needed them, but they'd spent theirs too soon. Carol was tempted to use more of her own money and buy the upstairs from her own company as an independent real estate venture. But the company would need the continuing income stream from those offices.

So she sold her Manhattan time-share and pulled out her six months' emergency money. With that and what she borrowed on her bonds, she committed another seven hundred thousand dollars to the plant. She welcomed the risk. This was her company, period. Yes, there was the matter of where she was going to live. She liked it here. She'd left New York. None of which had to do entirely with Easy Parsons, but she wanted that, too, to be where he was.

So then it was a financial relief for her that Remy split off the remodeled barn she was living in and sold it to a real estate investor in town who was also invested in the company and who could make sense of keeping Carol's rent low. She liked her little house, and she liked the graveyard behind the house. She'd toured the stones and now spoke nightly to Emily Ingersol, who'd outlived her husband, Jared, by forty years. Emily was a survivor. A lot of wives in the graveyard were survivors. Carol believed she was a survivor, and thinking that, she remembered again the names up the Town Hall stairwell. She reassured herself that times and boats had changed, and that everyone said Easy was a good fisherman. Somehow this was the first time that she'd thought of Easy being in danger. She'd begun to watch the weather. She started to understand how fortunate it would be to have Easy come here with his catches instead of to Boston. She felt his absences just in these two weeks and in all his trips out in the weeks and weeks to come.

Another piece of the puzzle, aside from keeping Easy alive and coming to her dock, was the setup for investors. Carol continued to have a back-and-forth with the redheaded numbers kid from Baxter Blume as he worked out the details of their stock plan, building it back from commitments by herself and Dave Parks and the rest as well as the meeting in the St. Peter's Club. When she told him she'd dumped some more money in, and how much it was, the kid asked Carol why she was doing it. Most people around Baxter Blume wouldn't imagine her relatively small investment, even now, could put anybody at the edge, but the redhead seemed to understand.

She wasn't going to talk to the kid about liking this town, much less about liking a man who fished out of the harbor. She told him she was committed to making her company go.

"Yeah, but why this company? You could have found a growth opportunity and leveraged it. You must be all in here, and what kind of return can you hope for?"

"I'm past fifty. I'm not looking to grow. I haven't got time for that. I want a company to run, and I want it now."

"But this company?"

"I like this company. I like this town. And as it happens there's a man here I like." She was ready to be sorry to have said all of that, except the kid was deaf to it.

"But you're risking like a twenty-five-year-old. And even I wouldn't do it."

She said, "I'm going to take that as a compliment. If we go belly-up, say nice things about me."

With the carelessness that smart kids can't hide, he said, "I'll always say nice things about the Beast."

When he wanted to pass judgment, Baxter wore nonprescription half-glasses so he could look over the tops of them at the offender. Carol didn't have half-glasses, but she was in her own plywood office, inside her own plant, in a town she was making her own, and she was old enough to be this boy's mother. She stood up, put her hands on her hips, and stared at him.

His chalk face flushed, and he said, "I'm sorry, Carol. Ms. MacLean. I will never call you that again."

She believed him, and she wondered if the name, if the Beast, really was done for good. She wondered if she would miss it. It had been useful once in a while. She hoped Beauty would become a name Easy might use sometimes, but she didn't want it to be more than that.

As soon as the company offices were complete, and the final sanitizing of the lines done, there were operational materials to lay in and staff shifts to schedule and low-hanging markets for their product to nail down.

The final task that had to be addressed on the property was the big backup cold-storage unit. It was a last priority, because inside the plant itself was a relatively new, relatively efficient, and relatively small cold storage with which they could run close to just-in-time and still have a measure of safety against a missed delivery on the blocks of frozen fish that fed the lines. This storage also had room to handle any surplus of catch or fillet from the new fresh business.

The old cold-storage building was a wild card they hadn't decided what to do with. It had been out of service for years, and no one had recently opened the door. Carol thought they might be able to gut it and put in another suite of offices to lease, but it wasn't clear how that would fly with the zoning board. They'd gotten away with leasing the floor above the plant because those offices were already in place.

Nobody could find the key to the old building, so Carol and Annette had the lock cut. There was a tight little entry office in which they could hear a hum, then a weighted insulation door, the large levered handle of which was cool. They pulled the door open to a wall of cold.

The backup, out-of-service cold storage was in service, and Annette and Carol said at the same time, "Here's the missing electricity."

Inside the cold storage was a mass of individually frozen fish, not blocks, carefully packed and layered on pallets. The storage space was filled wall to wall and nearly to the ceiling.

Carol was shy to bother him when he'd just gotten back, but she called Easy and told him about the fish and asked if he'd take a look. She hadn't seen him for a full two weeks while he was out on the water. Tonight was their official first dinner date, the one Easy had asked her for that evening at the St. Peter's Club. On the phone today, he said the boat was already clear and tight and the crew gone. He was glad he had a reason to come right over.

Buddy was in port, and he came along with Easy, and when the two of them arrived, Carol shook Buddy's hand so she'd get to shake Easy's, which he figured out and grinned about; they were both too shy for hugs.

Before going in the building, Buddy and Easy were casual about whatever the fish would turn out to be.

When they got out of the building, they were not casual.

Buddy said, "Patagonian toothfish."

Carol needed more than that.

Easy said, "Chilean sea bass."

Easy and Buddy went back in, and the next time out, they were prepared to guess it could be two million dollars' worth of Patagonian toothfish.

Carol thought they were putting her on.

"Illegal, toothfish," Easy said. "Illegal and going on extinct—that's why it's valuable."

The toothfish, Carol learned, was so near extinct that fishing for it was extraordinarily restricted around the world. Which made it profitable for pirate boats to run the restrictions, poach the fish, and sell it under the table wherever and to whomever they could.

It didn't take long for her to figure out what had happened. Mathews and his fat boys had bought a shitload of toothfish, almost certainly illegal, with money skimmed from the company. There were no records of any purchases in any books

Annette had seen. But it turned out the fat boys had made their toothfish legal in separate books kept in the antechamber of the storage building. Carol and Annette ran through the books in a couple minutes. Elizabeth Island's Best, which had bought all plant assets, owned two million dollars' worth of laundered toothfish. That two million had not been enough to persuade Mathews to buy the plant under harbor zoning, but it would have paid plenty of greens fees if he had been able to flip the site to a developer. For Carol, two million dollars meant more than greens fees. It didn't mean she could relax, but it did mean she wasn't completely naked in the storm. Her company was going to make it, and she had decided on that without a clue about toothfish. With an extra two million dollars, she would not have to be holding her breath for the years it was going to take the company to prove out. She took a breath, and she relaxed, and as soon as she did those things, she toughened back up. In the neighborhood where Carol was raised, you learned that if you got something extra, you were going to need it, and you'd better pay attention.

Easy said, "How do we do the right thing?"

His voice had an edge that surprised Carol. She let that go and focused on managing what she could. She said to Annette, "The electricity is billing through the new plant, isn't it?"

Annette said, "Yes, Remy might shut it off. I'll call him."

"And would you ask Parks to come over?"

Annette took Carol's cell and turned away, and Carol and Easy and Buddy stood facing the cold storage.

"It doesn't belong to Mathews anymore," Easy said. "But I wish we could put him in prison for it."

It was early in the day and they all stood in shadow, but the sun was enough above the main plant to light the corrugations at the top of the storage unit. The fat boys' industrial padlock hung on its open hasp beside the outer door. Carol could smell harbor, and the sunlight began to glare as it levered down the wall. She wouldn't have minded helping Mathews to jail, but toothfish wasn't the ticket; that would mean the fish was announced as officially illegal, and lost to Elizabeth Island's Best. No, Carol thought, the company needed the value of that fish. She could have laughed about two million dollars in free money.

Buddy said, for Carol's benefit, "We all caught too many fish, and if we could have, we'd have caught every one. But now most of us are trying to do it right. Because this is how we live, not just how we make a living."

Carol wasn't sure what that meant, but Buddy seemed to need to say it. She said, "Okay."

"Twenty years ago," Easy said, "people were buying boats for us."

He said that with his edge again. Carol thought she was falling in love with Easy, and she didn't understand how he could be so sharp with her. She said, "What's that have to do with us?"

Buddy said, "It's the background for that meeting in the gym at the high school. You wouldn't have known, but everybody there did, whether they admitted it or not. When the government pushed territorial fishing limits out to two hundred miles and gave the best grounds to Canada, then the government started big-time discount loaning on big boats for us, as good as telling us to go catch the last fish. So we did. We tried. And we made money. We did the fishing. We also paid the price. The fish and the money dried up, and most of the captains who didn't sink their boats for insurance, or bring in drugs, they ate their loans and left the water. Fifteen years ago, I'd let a lumper carry a haddock off over his shoulder when we were done unloading. Today, I watch every ounce comes out of my hold, and so does Easy."

Easy said, but without the edge now, "The question is, who's buying? And I don't mean at the supermarket."

Carol zeroed in on getting the history they were giving her, and what it meant to them—and to her, which was what seemed to be their point.

Buddy said, "Who's making the real money off of us? Who goes lobbying the government to loan on the bigger boats so they can make extra money off us? I caught the fish, and I'm paying the price. I ain't happy about it, but I'm living with it. We're all of us, the ones left, living with it."

"And we're bringing the fish stocks back," Easy said slowly, calm, no edge, but Carol could sense him not happy. "I didn't say it at the meeting in the gym, because we'd gotten what we needed and why fool with it, but if we could get the government to put observers on our boats and see what we see, they'd know for sure that we are bringing the stocks back. They send out research vessels to count fish, and the scientists don't know how to fish and don't know where to look. They're counting in the dark, and the guy driving the boat couldn't make it as a fisherman when fish were jumping into the ice."

"If we got real observers," Buddy said, "they'd see how much we pull in. They'd see how much we have to throw back that's over quota, that's bycatch. These are dead fish we're throwing back. But yeah, all right. If we have to pay for overfishing, all right, but let's really save the fish."

"And so then there's Mathews," Easy said to Carol, and the edge was back.

"So, what about Mathews?" Buddy said to her, looking at Easy to settle him down.

"What about this toothfish?" Easy said to her, not completely settled but not ugly.

Carol smiled at him, which wasn't the point, and was the point. She tilted her head toward the storage with its two million dollars' worth of stolen toothfish that by the time it went onto the menu would have to be worth closer to four million. She said, "Let me get this clear. The toothfish should never have been caught. That they were caught is a violation of the law and of what good fishermen are trying to do to save the ocean and make up for how they fished in the past. And this is Mathews's fault?"

"All the Mathewses," Buddy said, and now Buddy began to get angry.

Easy, holding back, but angry just the same, added, "Maybe it was American fishermen, maybe not."

Their anger had taken on personal intensity, and because she was the one in front of the anger, Carol was starting to get angry back. When she realized that, she looked down at Easy's boots and remembered those boots beside her that first night when she was on her hands and knees after Remy had told her she was out. She also remembered how she'd come to feel about Easy since then.

Besides which, she was a businesswoman and she could deal with a little heat.

"Whatever the last fish is worth," Easy said, "the Mathewses are going to find someone to go get it for them at a cost they can make money off of. After that, they start another business. Strip-mine the last of the shore and then develop it for second homes. When that's done, go into asbestos."

Carol, all common sense and business, love aside, said, "Mathews broke the law, apparently, but you're starting to make me feel like if I run a fish business, at the end of the day I'm wading through my own sewage just like Mathews." Which came out sounding harder than she meant, but they were coming at her.

Buddy said, as full-on angry now as if Carol were Mathews's right hand, "He was here, watching our days get cut, watching the fleet lose its boats and our kids take jobs in cubicles off the island. Meanwhile, he's buying fish nobody is allowed to catch. It's a fish outside our waters, but we've got plenty of illegal fish inside our waters, and we forfeit our boats if we catch them."

Easy looked almost as if he could take a swing. He said, "We're going to give this fish for charity or we're going to kill Mathews with it," and he looked hard at Carol. Still hard, he said, "We are not going to keep it."

Carol said, "We are going to keep it. I'm going to keep it." She knew what she was saying, and not just about the fish. She was telling Easy, the man she still had not kissed nearly enough, that she had other priorities. She'd be heartbroken in an hour or however long it took, but she'd say it again.

And she wasn't just thinking about her own invested savings. Every year of her life was in this company, the two million belonged to the company, and the company needed it. It was a fact that at least once a week she imagined herself among the legions of men and women she had fired. She hadn't gone in, and brought everybody else in, on a whim. If the business took too much longer than they'd hoped to get traction, at that point, two million dollars could mean everything. Carol believed Easy would understand eventually. It shouldn't have to be heartbreak between Easy and her company, Easy *or* her company.

Buddy said, "You're going to keep it?"

Annette had come back among them and heard most of it.

As Dave Parks jogged to them, he called, "Two million. No shit. But okay, who do we give it to? Start with the Coast Guard?"

"She's keeping it," Easy said. He said it and aimed it at her. "Dirty fish and dirty money and let the jerks go free."

At that, Carol damn near told him to hell.

"You're going to keep it?" Parks said.

Easy turned his back on the conversation. He looked away between the buildings at a slice of air over the harbor, and Carol felt the beginning of heartbreak, coming quicker than she'd have thought.

Buddy said, "We report the fish, and we say it was Mathews. Even if he's got the records to protect him, we make him look like who he is. And we look like who we are."

Easy didn't turn around.

Parks said, "Carol, Buddy may be right. It's a lot of money, but this is more sensitive than you know. The word will get out, and we'll be sleazebags. We don't want our new brand to say sleazebag. A lot of people in this town and down the coast, throughout the business, have been hurt by the restrictions. If we can say we're turning over illegal catch, if we can say we've got a real enough business that we can take the high road, it's going to make a difference. We're starting out and we're the little guy, but especially with what you just added in, we have the reserves to wait to be sleazebags until we're the big guy. Look at your investors. They don't want money from wiping out a species. I don't want it, and I'm not even a fisherman. Let's advertise it, Carol. Let's brand it. We're the company of the new fisherman, farming the ocean honestly and sustainably."

Carol concentrated on Parks. She heard him. She was doing what she had to do. She was doing her job. She said, "Fair enough, Dave." Then she turned to Annette.

Annette said, "We don't know if we'll make it, and we took money from people who can't afford to lose money. If the fish could swim, I would put them back in the water. Everybody we know is in this company, and some of them don't have jobs. They're our responsibility now. How we feel and how we look doesn't matter if we fail. Excuse me, Dave."

Buddy looked over the roof of the plant at a cloud of screaming gulls.

Carol said, "Thank you, Annette. For a moment, I'd almost managed to forget about the town money."

Parks said, "No need to excuse, Annette. We're having a meeting. We all say our piece, and Carol makes a decision."

Carol knew where Parks, Buddy, and Easy were coming from, and she believed that what Annette said might have the best chance of changing their minds. She did not believe Baxter would have to go through Annette's logic; Baxter, she was sure, would see that two million and pick it up before anyone else could blink.

She said to Parks, "Can we place it? Can what's left of our marketing department sell what we've got here? Our Chilean sea bass?"

Parks said, "Mathews would have fed it out a little at a time, and he would have had buyers lined up. We don't have those buyers lined up, and we don't have the logistics in place to slip out bits and pieces. If we try to sell in bulk, or if we put the word out to sell piecemeal, by the second day of trying to move this volume of illegal catch, some agency is going to be here suspending further sales until everything checks out. If Mathews did his fake books well enough, which he wouldn't have had to do if he knew his buyers, maybe we can hope to sell it all, but who knows how long that will take? In the best version, it'll get ugly and we'll get covered in mud, not to mention legal costs."

The cloud of gulls was moving away, following something, and Buddy watched them. Easy didn't move.

Annette said, "Buddy, your mother and her Wives of the Sea could sell those fish in an hour. And they would love to do it. And they're as much fishing people as you and Easy. After it's all sold, if anybody asks, we can say, truthfully, that we came by the fish honestly and that along with the fish we found books justifying the plant's original purchase of them."

Carol thought about the local fishermen's club and the diner, both named for Christ's fisherman, and it went back further than that. It went back to people nourishing themselves and their communities since the beginning of time. Buddy and Easy were standing up for oceans that had once seemed eternal, and for a way of life that had seemed equally eternal—and they were standing up against their own practical well-being. The new company Buddy and Easy had just invested in was nothing close to a sure thing, and the Patagonian toothfish could absolutely determine whether or not they lost everything. It was hard not to admire their integrity, and Carol did admire it.

She said to Annette, "Call Anna Rose and tell her and the Wives of the Sea to sell it all, and get immediate payment. If she has to give up on price to get payment, do it."

Annette still had the phone, and turned away to dial.

Carol said to Parks, "We start the first line in three days? Is that right?"

She knew it was right. She asked to find out if he was still on the team.

He said, "Everything's on schedule. And I wanted to tell you that what's left of marketing, which is a kid who used to work at the Chamber, is excited about cheese breading, a pizza-fish thing. Really, he's got some schools interested. He's thinking about prisons. He may be an asset, this kid."

She said, "I love the pizza-fish idea, Dave. I'll go to the schools with him, if you'll do the prisons. Annette, keep me posted on Anna Rose."

Then she turned and walked away from everyone. She walked away from Easy.

If she needed the two million dollars and didn't have it, if the company went under, she'd have to go back to shutting places and firing people, and she didn't even know if she could get hired for that again. Who would she be then? Not a CEO and not an undertaker. She tried to imagine Easy, standing behind her, but she could only see Dominic whom she'd loved from her hair to her toes and lost before anything. Since then she'd learned that she could live without love. Yet now, here was Easy, and it was as if she hadn't learned anything at all.

She kept walking. She had to keep walking.

Behind her, Parks sang just loud enough for her to hear, "There she goes."

Under her breath, Carol said, "Screw you, Parks." She walked away by herself and held her stomach. She'd chosen her company. She'd never have another chance.

Named Beauty

Easy turned around. She was walking away. He looked at Buddy, and Buddy looked back like he was thinking what a jerk Easy had been. Easy felt like he had said what had to be said, which he would say again in a heartbeat, and which, if you got down to it, he had not nearly said in the way he would have said to Mathews. With Mathews, it would have gotten beyond language. With Carol, he had only turned up the volume.

Easy told himself to come up for air. He liked that Carol was good at what she did. Maybe he even liked that she did what she had to do when it wasn't what he wanted. He was pretty sure he liked her, almost loved her, regardless of what she figured out about toothfish. He had started to think she felt the same way. He wondered if he wanted her to love him so much that she'd forget about her company.

Easy saw Carol MacLean walking away from him, and he called, "Beauty," and it came out a whisper. He called, "Carol."

She heard him. She walked away faster. She had business; she always had business—he admired that, but he believed what she was doing right now was leaving him, and god-damned Parks kept humming.

He said, "Jesus, Dave."

Parks said, "Jesus yourself, Easy. What's the matter with you? That's your girl."

Easy yelled, "Beauty!" and ran after her. He ran scared.

He'd run after Angie after she died. He hadn't been able to stop himself. He couldn't stop himself now either. He didn't want to stop. He should have started running after Carol the night he first saw her.

He ran so fast, he went past her and had to stop and then had to jog to stay beside her, because she could walk that fast. That was one more sweet thing about her. He could tell her that. He knew she had noticed him, but she was acting like she hadn't. He laughed because she wasn't going to laugh, and laughing was what Angie had taught him of love. He said, "I hope you weren't listening to Parks."

He didn't expect she'd look at him, and he was sure she wouldn't say anything, but he kept along next to her so she'd understand that he was going to keep it up.

Since he could only keep it up for so long before they got into the plant, he stepped in front of her and spread his arms so she had to stop and look at him. It had been a long time since he'd wished he was handsome, but he wished it now, not that he thought it would have made a difference.

He said, "Parks was singing that at me. You were leaving, and I wasn't paying attention. I wasn't getting it. He's guessed that I like you, and he was telling me that, 'There she goes,' and if I liked you, I'd better run after you."

She moved to go around him, and he stood in front of her again.

He said, "You think I can't accept a decision? I'm a captain. I drive a sizable boat and run a crew. I take responsibility for that boat and those people, and if those people don't do what I say, the boat's in trouble. You drive this company. I respect that."

That wasn't what he'd meant to say at all. Or it wasn't the most important thing. The most important thing was what Parks had guessed.

She looked past him and said, "Right now I've got carpenters framing the lunchroom and setting in lockers." She was beautiful outdoors, not that she wasn't beautiful indoors.

He said, "I'm sorry I sounded angry. I was angry, but not at you. You were there, so it came at you. I was a jerk to you, and I'm crazy sorry for that. I ain't happy about the toothfish, but it's your decision, and it's done. I'm at my oar." And that wasn't what he meant to say either.

She said, "Thank you, Easy," and moved to go around him again, slower though, a good sign. He could walk and keep up beside her.

"You know what this means?" he said.

He wondered if she thought because he was still angry at her and she was angry at him that there was no going back. He'd never been angry at her, though he knew he'd sounded that way. Then Parks had started singing. It wouldn't be hard at all to tell Carol that she meant more to him than toothfish.

Carol said, "Tell me what it means, Easy."

He said, sounding as sure of himself as he could, "Finding the toothfish means we can afford to take a day off."

It was a Friday morning. He had the boat cleaned up, and they were supposed to go to dinner. He bet she'd forgotten about that. He said, "And dinner. Remember?"

She said, "You expect me to believe Parks was singing at you?"

"Of course he was. He wouldn't needle you like that." Easy took a deep breath. This was what he had to say, and he said it so she'd have to understand. "Parks gets it how much I like you."

He took hold of her arm with both of his hands. She didn't pull her arm away. He said, "Once you open the doors of that place, we won't have another chance for months."

Easy was ready for her to tell him to let go, but he had to hold on. They were at the door into the plant and he turned her away and kept on walking.

He said, "I want you to take the day on my boat. You should know, in your business, how a stern dragger drives."

They walked all the way around to his boat without either of them saying anything more. He kept both his hands on her arm as if she might run away, and he looked at her the whole time.

He let go for the climb down onto his boat and up again into the pilothouse. She followed. It wasn't anything difficult, but he was glad she had on flat shoes. Then when she was up in the pilot-house, he found himself wondering why she didn't ever wear high heels. She had nice legs, even in her suits with pants.

He started the engine and untied and backed out. She stood beside him at his wheel.

When you first pulled into the inner harbor and shut down and the air was still, the smell of fish could be strong, but the guys had hosed down, and he and Carol would soon be to the outer harbor. He feathered his engines and played the wheel. It was something he did every day, short radius changes of direction, the slides, but Carol was watching closely, and he remembered picking up that she was a car person, or had been as a kid. So he took his boat into the channel for the thousandth time and felt like he was showing off.

It was a beautiful day. Briny wind, the sky as blue as God,

the sides of the cabin open, and already they were to the outer harbor. He throttled up, and he could tell she was listening to the good engines that he had in the boat and that he kept good. Easy always liked what he did, but it was work, and when you were working, you took things for granted. Today, he felt like Carol would feel, the boat underfoot and the water carrying the boat.

She looked past him at the mansions of the richest summer people, along the shore of Eastern Point. She stood close enough that their elbows were firm against one another. There wasn't any kind of swell, no roll to the boat, but maybe she wanted to be ready, and he wasn't going to argue. He liked having her near.

She looked through his salted windshield, squinting into the glare off the water. Ahead was the breakwater, and outside, the ocean rolled with swells. They weren't big, but Easy wasn't going to take her outside anyhow.

She looked at him now. She seemed about to say something important but she didn't say it; she just looked.

So he said, to his windshield in his pilothouse, "When I was a kid, I joined the Army, and they sent me to the South. I followed a girl to the Mississippi coast, and we got married and were happy head to toe, and she died with our baby giving birth. Long time since. That's the only other woman I ever felt this way about."

He hadn't planned to say that about Angie, but he believed it was the kind of thing people who loved one another talked about. He realized he'd also pretty much told Carol that he loved her, not just liked but loved, and he hadn't planned that either, though he felt as if he'd been trying to say it all morning.

He glanced over at Carol. She was staring at him as hard as if her life depended on it, but she looked deaf.

"Oh no," he said. "Stand outside on the deck. Hold to the rail."

She didn't move. She mumbled about liking his cabin, but she was looking again at the swells beyond the breakwater.

He spun his wheel, and the boat turned in a slow, weighted slide to aim back toward town. Then he got her out of the pilothouse. She didn't have time to make much of a mess on his deck, a deck that had seen a lot worse messes. Most of it went over the rail, and she said, "I'm sorry."

Easy held her with one arm all the way around her waist. With his other hand he kept her hair clear. He liked holding her, but he could think of better times to do it. He wasn't going to blame her that she got seasick. It happened. But it was as if he'd never told her he loved her.

She retched, and he braced her sideways against his leg and his hip. She hung over the rail and asked in a tiny voice, "Who's steering?"

He should tell her again, just say it, but probably not now. It couldn't be good to say you love somebody while she's vomiting, though that was probably better than telling her and having her vomit as soon as she heard.

Still holding to the rail, she stood up and looked down herself. It was on her shoes.

He couldn't possibly tell her now. He handed her the handkerchief from his back pocket. It was clean. He said, "You may need some new shoes." He said it in fun, to distract her. He'd had sick people on the boat, out for day rides. Sometimes a joke helped. "Does this mean you don't like cruising on a ninety-two-foot Elizabeth Island stern dragger?"

She said, "I'm fine."

She wiped her mouth and couldn't seem to decide what to do

with the handkerchief, so she threw it over the side. He didn't care about the handkerchief, but he said, "Why don't you throw the shoes, too. Come on. Get some new shoes."

She said, "I should get back to work."

He drove the boat and she waited for shore.

He tried to help her get off, and she shrugged him away. When she was off, she looked and saw, for the first time he guessed, the name of the boat.

She said, "Your boat is named *Beauty*."

"If that's what it says."

He was mad, and he sounded mad, and that wasn't fair to her. She was the one who'd thrown up; she was supposed to get mad, not him. She was walking away again, and he had to run after her again and begin all over. He wanted to. He didn't blame her for walking off. He tied the boat in a hurry, terrified he wouldn't catch her.

He ran after her shouting, "I'm sorry, I'm sorry, I'm sorry," wishing he could say, "I love you, I love you, I love you."

Heels

Carol didn't feel queasy anymore, and she was not so weak she couldn't walk. She looked back once to be sure the name of his boat was what she'd seen, but she couldn't tell because he was running up with his *sorry*s as if she still needed help. Hardly touching her, which was more than she wanted, he guided her to his truck and opened her door, and as soon as she got in, she was glad not to be walking. She would have been glad even if she weren't covered in vomit. She was also glad they didn't speak. Before she threw up, he had as much as said he loved her. She wished she felt more excited. Today, her company was almost open for business, and they'd wandered into a couple million dollars of free fish, and Easy Parsons had said he loved her. But right now, she couldn't wait to get out of his truck and away from him.

She looked out the window and didn't understand why he was going the long way around, down Main Street. She felt like she was emptied of everything, including anger, and she wondered if he would be able to say he loved her again.

He double-parked on Main Street, put down her window, leaned across her, and called to a group of women going in Elizabeth's expensive restaurant for lunch. He called, "What're the best women's shoes?" The women curled their shoulders and pushed at the restaurant door. Carol sank down in her seat like an embarrassed teenager, and Easy shouted at the women in the voice of someone picking a fight. "What are the best women's shoes in the damn world?"

"Manolos," one of them said over her shoulder, and Easy turned around to stare at whoever had honked behind the truck.

Carol told him, "You aren't going to find Manolos anywhere near Elizabeth."

"So they are good?"

"I know that much."

"I'm getting you Manolos. My boat makes you sick, I replace the shoes."

"I'm changing my clothes and going back to the plant."

"What, are you too embarrassed to go into Boston, into a flashy store, with one of your company's fishermen?" At which point he left the truck where it was and ran into Elizabeth's one expensive restaurant and came out with the name of a store in Boston called Harry's.

He let her change her clothes, and she was tempted to run out the back of her place and through the graveyard, past Emily Ingersol, to get away. Only now she wasn't sure she wanted to get away. She put on a skirt instead of pants.

⅄

Harry's was four stories of Boston brick at the fancy end of Newbury Street, and if it had only been expensive, she would have been fine—Manolos she guessed would run seven or eight hundred dollars, which she hoped would be enough to make Easy regret his project. But after he pushed open the door and Carol walked in, it was clear that Harry's was more than just expensive. It was the height of chic. And Carol was too tall and too plain, a plague on chic.

Easy tugged her toward a young and beautiful saleswoman and shouted, "We need a pair of heels."

Carol wanted to apologize for him. She also wanted to hide her feet, but the saleswoman would not look at them anyway.

Easy said, "Manolos."

The saleswoman heard that and gazed at Carol's feet. It was the kind of change Carol had seen when people didn't realize at first who Baxter was. She was amazed to find herself thinking of Baxter, though of course he shopped in places like this.

The saleswoman said, "Yes," slowly and thoughtfully appreciating Easy's decision.

The saleswoman said to Easy, "Come this way," and smiled. She said, "I'm Amanda." She was very pretty, and Carol, who was not pretty, didn't believe she was entitled to follow along. She was ready to give up and tell Easy to go on with Amanda by himself.

Easy, in his khaki pants that were clean but not pressed and his denim shirt that had its pocket beginning to tear loose, said with quiet authority, "Glad to meet you, Amanda." It was the delivery of somebody who could buy the building, and it surprised Carol and perked her up a little bit and got another look from Amanda.

Carol was a little over six-one and would be taller than that in heels. She held her shoulders back and followed Amanda and Easy into a room that looked nothing like any shoe department she had ever seen. She sat and let Amanda remove her flats so that anybody including Easy could look at her naked feet. Carol looked at the ceiling, which was high and elegant.

She continued to look at the ceiling when she stood to have her feet measured. She sat back down and ignored the styles of shoes Amanda showed her; she pretended to be someone who had other people choose such things, and then she hated herself for playing along with the store's snobbery.

Amanda took hold of her foot, and the touch was so intimate Carol got clammy, and then the first pair, when she stood up, hurt Carol's feet, and she said so and was glad she didn't have to look. She sat back down without looking at Easy either. She wouldn't have looked at anybody if the room had been packed.

The heels on the second pair were so high that if Carol didn't have good balance and strong legs and strong feet she wouldn't have been able to walk. She could walk, though, and the shoes didn't hurt. They felt all right. She walked to the grand, old Boston window and looked above opulent cars to Newbury Street. The window and the elegant ceiling made the contemporary chic of the store more chic.

She looked down.

They were red shoes, and she was already proud of herself for being able to walk in them. She was proud of the courage it would take to wear them out of the store. She hoped they did cost a gazillion.

She turned to Easy now and said, "Okay? Are we done?"

Easy sat in a plush armchair as solidly as if he belonged in the Harry's shoe room. Or at least he looked as if he knew who he was regardless of where he was. She guessed he had known that in more difficult places than Harry's. He looked at her and didn't say a thing about the Manolos he was so determined to inflict on her, so she turned back toward the window and pulled up the skirt she had worn in anticipation of his god-damned shoes. She pulled it up far above her knees, and turned around in a circle twice and faced him again.

Easy leaned forward in his chair and grinned and said, "We'll take them."

She liked his grin. She knew that shoes were not going to make her any prettier than she already was. But these shoes made her stiff posture feel more graceful.

Also, Easy's grin was sexy and made her feel sexy.

She walked to the mirror and looked at Easy in the reflection and said, "Thank you." He looked back at her in the mirror and down to the shoes and back up at her, and he didn't lose his grin. You would have thought he was the one who was able to stand up and walk in the shoes. "I love my shoes, Easy," she said. And then, not exactly out of the blue, "I want a dress to go with them."

He said, "Good."

She faced him and said, "I'll buy the dress."

He said, "Better," and stood up out of his chair as if he hadn't forgotten he could buy the building, and Carol laughed.

Amanda, whom both of them had nearly forgotten, said, "Yes," slowly and discerningly, speaking to Carol now.

Up the grand staircase, shamelessly playing along with Harry, Carol said, "Something to have a martini in." Carol figured if she were going to make a fool of herself, she should do the full nine yards. Maybe she'd actually have a martini. Amanda got them near what might have been dresses and looked at Easy, and Easy was shy. Shoes had been his limit.

Amanda was ready. She said, "Von Furstenberg."

It wasn't as if Carol had never read a women's magazine. It just had never occurred to her to wear the clothes. Now she missed Easy's authority. Carol nodded, and Amanda gathered three or four dresses. One of them was navy with a bit of red piping, and Carol worried that navy was the color of the suits she had already, but this dress was short, and the fabric was nice and would hang well. She thought the red piping would work with her shoes. She took it to the dressing room.

She looked at herself in the mirror in her own suit, and she was who she was. She took off the suit, and in her underwear, she was who she was, not awful, but hard to imagine as a prize. She was all bone and elbows and knees, without even a chest to speak of.

She put on the new dress, and she was still who she was, and for a moment she was disappointed. She had not expected to be different, but she had hoped.

Amanda called, "Carol. Come look in a mirror out here. The light is so much better."

As soon as she heard that, she realized her knees. They were below the hem of the dress, and they glowed like blue knobs in the dressing room light, uglier than God ever imagined. She pulled open the door and ran from the dressing room before she chickened out.

When she'd gone in the dressing room, Easy had been standing by a chair. He had not moved since. He stood there and looked at her, and she was paralyzed. She could not make herself walk around. She could not make a model's pose, whatever that would have been. She smiled at him. She could do that. She loved him. She believed he loved her. He was smart and strong and capable and did real work and was kind and believed in his life, and no matter what she thought about herself, he thought she was pretty.

She looked over at Amanda for a clue, but Amanda was watching Easy, and now Amanda was preening like she'd won something Carol had no idea about. Carol looked at Easy again, and he was trying to sit into the chair and had missed and gotten the arm of the chair and now slipped off that into the seat.

Amanda said, "I think that's a yes."

Easy righted himself in the chair and grinned again like with the shoes, only more. Carol could feel his hands everywhere the dress touched her.

He said, "Jesus, Carol."

⅄

Amanda wrapped Carol's old clothes in tissue and hid them in a chic bag and said where to go for a cocktail.

After Carol and Easy had sat for an hour with their one martini apiece, laughing about Harry and Amanda, the bartender said where to go for dinner—Italian, crusty bread, white tablecloths, candles and waiters in long aprons.

When they reached their table, Carol asked the waiter to go away and stood beside Easy and said, "I heard you on the boat, about being married, about losing her and your baby, about how much you loved her. I'm sorry. I'm glad you had love like that, so much that it could last and last, and I'm sorry she died and your baby."

Then she sat down in her beautiful dress and her electric shoes, and Easy sat down across from her, and she might as well have been naked. She loved Easy Parsons, and if he had had joys and if he had hurt, she loved those things, and she loved that he had offered them to her. She said, "Forgive me for saying it now, when we're supposed to be having fun." Even if she hadn't answered his offer just right or at the right time, still she wanted to have met it.

"Thank you for saying so."

Carol, naked, went ahead. She said, "The boy I loved got killed in Vietnam. We weren't married, but we would have, and we loved each other, and even then, I knew I'd had the love I was going to have. After he died, all that was left was work. So I worked harder."

The waiter opened her napkin in her lap, and Easy just looked at her.

"His name was Dominic. We did cars in the alley behind our houses. It was a neighborhood outside Detroit where in the spring men with stomachs hosed the soot off their houses that were pastel colors like the sunsets over the plants."

Easy shrugged and nodded and shook his head and leaned down at his place on the table. Like he was shy to say whatever it was. The waiter laid Easy's napkin beside his elbow.

He looked up at her and said, "I could always catch fish."

This was what he was shy to say? Carol didn't know if she could laugh.

He said, "Seriously, from when I was little. I could catch so much it was unfair. Not to the fish. I mean for other kids then, and for other fishermen now. It's embarrassing unless it's what you do. Also, it lets me see sunsets and all kinds of other light on the ocean."

Carol said, keeping a serious voice, "Would you take me out and show me? I have shoes that have been on boats."

Easy laughed and so did she, and she was more pleased than she would have thought possible.

But when she stood up to go to the bathroom, the waiter stared, and that fast she was self-conscious about her dress and her shoes and her height and not being pretty enough for anything but a blue suit.

But Easy saw the waiter look and said, "Back off, pal," like the waiter had been looking her up and down, and maybe he had. A couple at the next table seemed startled by Easy's tough voice, but Carol could tell he had been kidding, and the waiter laughed, and Easy laughed, and Carol went in a strut toward the bathroom.

When she got back, Easy said, "Do you want to get a hotel room?"

She was in business with Easy. In fact, a critical part of the business, the fresh fish that would be her profit margin, the success or failure of the business, really, depended on Easy. Shouldn't she have a position on that? Wasn't there a relationship code about behaving sensibly around the people you worked with? She knew perfectly well there was, and she'd never had to pay the least of attention. She very nearly laughed at the notion. She'd been burying dead companies forever, and she'd done that alone, and none of the guys she'd fired would have wanted to ask her. But now, she had her own company, a living company. Carol MacLean. And she had a man right here who wanted to go to bed with her. She stood beside him and let him look her up and down for real to be sure. She said, "What's the best hotel?"

It wasn't a big room, but it was very nice, and it looked over the Public Garden. She sat on the edge of the bed in her dress and her shoes. She was more nervous than in the restaurant but happy. She was who she was, and right now that had everything to do with the man in the room, who sat down beside her and told her to close her eyes. He put his thumb to her lips and whispered, "Beauty."

Obituary

Baxter had pulled out of Blume's new fund and was thrilled to be out and wished them all well. He had some ideas that he was not ready to talk about much less do anything about. He had time on his hands. He flipped through the obituary section, something he'd begun early in his career, thinking he might get a leg up on a promising turnover coming into play, and actually once it had paid off. This was how habits began.

And now, just when he was at loose ends and wanted something to dabble with, he came upon an interesting death. It was the head of a third-generation family company, hopelessly complicated (family and company both). The name had come across low on his radar enough times for Baxter to know that the company had a few interesting pieces. One piece in particular had marginal value to anyone else but was something he might put to use. He had some discreet calls made, made some discreet follow-up calls himself. There wouldn't, in the bigger picture, be much money involved. It was a New

England company, logging, once upon a time. Why not? So, Boston, the Four Seasons.

And last night, over dinner with some of the family, he had found himself in a swamp of competing hopes and hatreds that made his own family look like a Hallmark card. They wanted something besides money, something that sat on the ground and made a product, though he thought some of them, for sentimental reasons, would have preferred something that only used to make something. Baxter had had such things pass through his stewardship in the past but didn't have one at the moment. He could put people on it for a few hours, but the family wanted a deal done today. This was what dabbling could lead to.

Baxter was an early riser and he went down to the lobby for a paper, not really thinking lightning could strike through the obits so soon again, but you never knew.

He was surprised and happy to see this headline over a column on the bottom half of the front page:

STUDY MOURNS OCEAN, FAULTS FISHING

Judge Imposes Punishing Regs

Surprise

In the morning, Easy Parsons was the happiest man on land or sea, and he went down to the lobby early to get toothbrushes and then went out on the street so the day could meet him and he could breathe it in.

Coming back in through the lobby, he grabbed a paper and thought that he loved Carol because she was beautiful, which was stupid to think right off, but she was. He also loved her because she walked fast, and even though she was shy, which he liked, she could take charge when necessary. She was working people. She knew that he was a working guy who needed the sea and whose boat was a factory. He loved that she knew what he did and that he loved it. He was sure she could learn to find fish if they were ten years old together.

He loved that she went ahead with the shoes and then the dress, and he loved that she let him put his face into her beautiful red hair, and when she kissed, despite how stiff she could seem when she was walking fast, she kissed as soft as any creature under God's blue heaven.

Then he saw the headline.

In the elevator, he tried to get control. Nobody had died. In two weeks, when the new regs went into effect, he could no longer catch fish in New England. He would have to take the boat south to Christ only knew where, which meant he would not be with Carol. There wouldn't be any fresh fish coming in or any fishermen left to bring it, and fresh fish was what Carol's plant needed. She had skills, and she wouldn't want to give up, but even with the extra two million, her plant was dead in the water. Carol would know that and she would pull the plug right away, get out what money she could, and spread that around town.

And then Carol would have to go back to New York, where she could make a living. Maybe she could get her own job back. There wouldn't be room for Easy in her New York program. She would be who she used to be, and he would be who he used to be, and that guy he used to be felt like he was dying. He'd barely met her, and now he couldn't live without her, and he was going to lose her.

It wouldn't take her long, he figured, to shut and empty the plant. If he stuck around after the regs kicked in, everything would just get harder. With every extra day they would both know they were a day closer to the end of it. Would he sit on his boat and watch the plant? Would she look out at him while she worked her phone unloading the lines? Would they hold each other every night hurting more and more? That couldn't be fair. He could stand anything, but he couldn't bear to think of Carol hurting any more than she had to.

Don't drag it out, he thought. He would take his crew fishing for every nickel they could catch in two weeks, and then he would head back out—south it would have to be. If there was any kindness he could still do for Carol, it had to be that he would just go.

In the elevator, he kept in control, and when the doors opened, he was able to walk.

Carol was in her business suit down the hall outside their room with a guy who looked like he was dressed for weekend Monopoly. Sport coat too smooth even for a sport coat, and suit pants, loafers with tassels, yellow socks. The jerk was holding the newspaper.

Easy concentrated on Carol. He held up his paper. He said, "Remember the judge who put off the tough fishing regulations two weeks ago? Yesterday she changed her mind." Lay it out, he told himself, keep it simple.

The other guy was nodding, but he took a step back. Carol knew. She had composed herself. She said, "The judge is enforcing the amendment to cut back your days and your catch and where you can go." She looked like she had taken the punch and gotten her breath back. Carol would be all right. "It's fixable," she said.

It wasn't fixable, and Easy wanted to get it over with as fast and painlessly as he could, for her sake. He reached her and said, "Every ground fisherman north of Delaware is losing another sixty-five percent of their days. We're not going to be able to feed your plant, and we're not going to be able to feed ourselves."

She said, "Easy, listen." He had to hand it to her. She sounded like emergency was her bread and butter. She'd have made a good captain.

Last night was more than he'd ever hoped for. But he had to go. "The regulations take effect in two weeks. I'm going to fish those days for my crew, and then look for new water."

Carol said, "At the gym, you told people your boat could survive the new regulations."

"That was noise, and in the gym I told you so. Nobody wins derby fishing. I didn't want the bureaucrats to think they were throwing a bone to a bunch of half-wits."

Easy didn't like the anger that had jumped into his voice, but maybe it was just as well.

Carol said, "Easy, we can handle this," and said it like how she'd said she loved him, last night, which he'd said to her and meant with all his heart, and now his heart was beside the point, and he was doing what he had to do.

He said, "I'm going to call my crew. I'll pay the room and leave you taxi money downstairs. But I want to tell you something."

She looked at the jerk businessman like she didn't want him to hear, and she closed her eyes. As if she thought he was going to tell her he loved her again. That was what Easy wanted to tell her, but he couldn't and he wouldn't. That was the whole point. Don't drag it out. Not fair to her.

He said, "You were right to keep the two million. When you go under, try to get my crew their investment back. I don't need anything back on my own investment. If I need more to set up somewhere else, I can borrow on the boat. Remember the little guys."

He couldn't bear to listen to himself, and neither could Carol. She didn't open her eyes. She squeezed them tight shut and tighter, like he had hit her, and he had.

He said, "I've got to go. Here's a toothbrush for you. I got toothbrushes before I saw the paper."

He took her hand and put the plastic container for a toothbrush in it, and she kept her eyes shut, so he had to fold her fingers over the toothbrush. They were a stranger's fingers now, and yet he knew them.

He began to back away, but before he turned around, the jerk said, "I'm Tom Baxter. I'm a principal in what people call a private equity firm, a buyout firm."

"Good for you," Easy said. He said, "Carol, remember the little guys."

He turned and headed for the elevators. He was getting shut out of his home and his harbor and the fishing grounds that he knew and that fed him and his crew. He was getting shut away from Carol. If it would have helped, he would have given up his boat, and that was a discussion you had with God when you were going to change the shape of wind, and even so he would have done it. Instead he did what you did when the trouble was too much—you did the next thing and the next. Easy took one step at a time back to the elevators.

The Baxter guy called down the hall after him. "I'm here to buy Elizabeth Island's Best. If you're an investor, you're one of the people I'll be writing a check to. You and your crew."

Easy stopped and looked back. Carol had opened her eyes, but it was Baxter who had the wheel.

"I'm prepared to pay a very good price," Baxter said to Easy, a conversation voice now. "A significantly better price than you and your men and the rest of the town paid."

Easy walked back to him and said, "You're Baxter Blume. I get that part."

"I was in town for work and saw today's paper and realized I might have a deal that could work for everybody. I spent some time tracking down Carol and came over to make an offer. Unless I miss my guess, you were going to catch the fresh fish for Elizabeth Island's Best profit margin. I was very sorry to see the paper. I'm sorry for the dislocation of your business as a fisherman. I'm sorry for your crew."

Baxter offered his hand, and Easy shook it. You didn't get

to be a successful jerk unless you had skills, and Baxter had the sense not to pretend to be a blue-collar fat-ass from the docks. He talked in his overeducated jerk voice straight at Easy, doing business man-to-man as if Easy were in charge.

Well, he was in charge of doing what he could for his guys. And you didn't become a successful fisherman just by catching fish. When you brought your catch in, if you were good and consistent, you made deals, and Easy had found that if you had what people wanted, you did best keeping your mouth shut.

It seemed like Baxter was waiting for Easy to say something, and when Easy didn't, Baxter went ahead. "We can make you more than whole. We can, at the very least, get you what you need to set up in new waters, as you say. You'll probably set up on your own, the way that suits you. But it's not impossible I could also help with that, and if you let me know where you're going, I'll certainly make some calls."

Easy didn't give a damn about himself at this point. He did care about his crew and Buddy and Buddy's crew and Buddy's family and everybody else on Elizabeth Island. Those were his people. He watched Baxter and waited. He hadn't heard anything resembling a trustable offer, and he wasn't going to count on the "making calls" bullshit.

He was startled when Carol spoke. She said, "Easy wants to know why you want the company, Baxter, and whether he can count on your money."

Easy couldn't care less about the money for himself. Didn't she know that? He ought to be angry at her if she didn't know that. For some reason, he was angry at himself. You couldn't be angry at the paper. He concentrated on Baxter.

Baxter said to Easy, "Carol, can you tell Easy why I'm here and whether I'm good for my commitments?"

Carol sounded like she was getting angry, too. At Easy?

She said, "You guys know whose company this is?" But she was talking to Baxter, and Easy wasn't sure where he fit in. She said, "You're doing what you do, Baxter. My guess is that you're trying to get hold of a large family company around here, or some hunk of it. You're close to making the deal. This weekend. When you saw the article in the paper and knew we'd have to sell our little company, you also knew that the owners of your big company might make the deal if you could show up today with a box of chocolates in exactly the shape of our company. It is today, isn't it? Otherwise why are we here? But why do they want us? Maybe they can afford to wait for the zoning. Can they work conservation easement trade-offs? Even if you pay us too much, your price on our property will be nothing compared to the long-term tax basis they can assign. Am I close?"

Carol was going to sell the company, and Easy figured this was how she meant to negotiate it. If she could get all of the investors in town all of their money back, that was great under the circumstances. If people made a profit, even better. If Easy got included in the profit, fine, but as far as he was concerned, everything was still a wreck. He was going south. He and Carol had had one day. What he couldn't figure was why he was even here in the hall, with Baxter talking at him and Carol looking from him to Baxter to him to Baxter.

"She knows her stuff, Easy. I'd like to be able to promise your plant to some folks, and I'd like to be able to promise it today."

Easy had started to feel ashamed of himself for pretending he had a right to discuss any kind of deal for Carol's company, but he kept going because here he was. He said, "What are you promising us?"

Carol said, "Us?" like the word was a joke or a lie, and like maybe Easy was a joke and a lie, too.

That didn't sit well, but Easy knew she didn't want to lose her company. He knew she wasn't happy and that she was doing her best, hustling to save the investors regardless of hurt feelings. He admired that she was still that tough, even though Baxter buying the company, at whatever price, didn't put fish back in the ocean or change the judge's decision. It didn't keep Easy from going south, and Carol back to New York.

Baxter said to Easy, "We're prepared to pay you one hundred and fifty percent of your investment, including improvements. Which I wouldn't offer if I didn't want to get a commitment on this right now. I might, though, like to haggle for a few minutes about the proceeds on the Chilean sea bass which came up on the radar of one of my interns."

This time, Easy looked at Carol to see if he was supposed to say something. Every second since he had gotten off the elevator, he had gotten smaller and weaker and more beside the point. Since it was obvious about Easy and Carol, did Baxter want Carol to sell cheap because she liked Easy? Did that make sense?

Easy should have been grateful as hell that he was going to get his investment back, make money on it, leave his crew with something in their pockets before he drove south. But he was not grateful as hell. He had to be happy that he and Carol had met, but he wished to hell that they could be unmet now.

Carol looked at him, and he couldn't tell if she was heartbroken or if she'd already written him off. He hoped the new dress and the shoes would work in New York.

She said, "Easy, I'm sorry for you losing the fish and the grounds and the harbor you know."

She sounded professionally sincere. He could have been a gas station going out of business. Which was great, exactly what he wanted.

"Sorry doesn't reverse the judge," Baxter said, sounding a whole shitload more sympathetic than Carol. Easy was so far out of his league that all he could think was he had to get to open water.

He didn't say anything in answer to Baxter. He didn't plan on saying anything, period, until he got out of the hotel.

Baxter nodded as if he and Easy were in perfect agreement, and said, "Let's get Carol's take on the money before we go any further."

Then Baxter made a thing of turning to Carol.

Easy didn't bother. The money would be what it was and would make setting up somewhere else easier. He wished he thought that Buddy could come. But Buddy's and his father's boats had Elizabeth Island in their keels, and Buddy had a family of his own.

Baxter said, "What do you think, Carol? Is Baxter Blume good for it? If I can trust your commitment to the basics of a deal, Carol, can you trust me to find the money? So Easy can drive his boat to sea knowing that everyone on board has a bank account? I think you and I, Carol, both have an idea of the figures. Maybe Easy does, too."

What Easy knew was that the best thing he could do was never let Carol MacLean and Easy Parsons see each other again.

Carol said, so level it came out like a threat, "I don't own a majority of Elizabeth's Best, but I own a lot more than anyone else, and I'm confident I can put together a majority if it came to that, if you wanted to pursue it, Baxter."

Easy was so amazed at the danger in Carol's voice that at first he didn't get what she'd said.

Baxter said, "I'm not sure what you're saying, Carol."

Carol looked at Baxter and said, "The company is not for sale."

Easy didn't know the details like Carol, but he knew the company had to have fresh fish to make a go of it. That was the whole plan. Reaching the end of the rope, even with the toothfish money, would not take all that long.

She said to Easy and Baxter both, "I'm not going to sell it, and I'm not going to let you assholes sell it for me."

Easy, all of a sudden, was getting less tiny and weak and beside the point. Baxter looked calm as a seal in sun and smiled at Easy like they had a secret, as if now he thought that, because of Easy, Carol would never refuse a sale.

Easy could see that Carol wasn't surprised by Baxter's play. She'd worked with Baxter before. She faced Easy like he was the one she didn't know. She said, "I am sorry about the amendment, and I'm sorry if I disappoint you by refusing to sell to Baxter Blume. I plan on making the company go. If it doesn't go, I will do my best to look out for your crew." She could have been an out-of-town lawyer talking nice about boat repossession.

She was a businesswoman in a business that had just gone broke. If she didn't sell, she was sneaking into people's houses and setting their savings on fire. He guessed she would know about that. She didn't need to hear him say it.

As best he could tell, she had forgotten him. He must have been nuts to think he had to worry about her being heartbroken and about how he'd have to leave quick and clean so she didn't hurt too much from losing him. He was the one who hurt too much. She had her company. And she was ready to choose her precious company not just over him—who wouldn't understand that—but over every single investor to the last penny. She was choosing against a town, his town, his family and every other family named on the Town Hall stairs. Easy hated that, and he still loved her. Oh, man.

He left—what he should have done before he got in the elevator to come up.

Loaves and Fishes

Carol couldn't bear to watch him all the way to the elevators. Instead, she looked at Baxter, and wondered if he saw her differently now.

She heard the elevator.

Baxter seemed pleased to have gotten something wrong for a change.

He said, "Call me if you change your mind."

Then he dropped his newspaper outside someone else's door and walked away down the emptied hall.

Carol went in their room holding the toothbrush Easy had given her.

She put the toothbrush on the bedside table and sat on the bed and wept like an angry kid because it was so unfair. No matter what she did, Easy had to go. If she sold to Baxter, she could at least give all the investors, including herself, a nice profit. The town wouldn't hate her, and she could face her poor job prospects with money in the bank instead of broke. But that wouldn't keep Easy here. He couldn't fish here. He'd make money on his investment, but then what? He was a fisherman, and they both knew she was not. She couldn't ask him to come ashore and follow her. He belonged on the water. That was who he was and who she loved.

If it would have kept Easy, she would have sold to Baxter. But Baxter couldn't give her Easy, and if she couldn't keep Easy, she was going to keep her company. That was who she was. She cried because all she had was everything she'd ever wanted—her own company—and no matter how well she ran it, she would lose it in no time, exactly the same amount of time it would take her to lose the town's investments.

And she had managed to send Easy away mad, which probably was best. If he went away mad, he'd forget about her that much more easily. She cried because she couldn't do anything else, because Easy hated her and was right to hate her, and she'd made it that way.

She stood up and folded her new dress and put it in the Harry's bag with the Manolos.

She straightened the bed for no reason. She looked out the window over the early, sun-shined Public Garden that was opening into spring and had beds yellow with the first crocuses and forsythia. There was blue overhead.

Easy had paid for the room and left money for a cab. She used it. On the ride back to Elizabeth, she wondered how long her body would remember him. She closed her eyes to keep what she could.

人

She didn't go to the plant. She called Anna Rose Taormina and said, "May I come over?" Carol was not going to be at the plant while there was any chance of seeing Easy's boat.

Anna Rose said, "I'm across Lincoln from you and up eight houses on the left. Don't go to the side door. That's my oldest daughter and her boy now. Come in the front door and through to the kitchen."

Carol drove. It was a two-tone house, with a four-foot statue of Mary in a shell beside the step. Carol parked looking uphill and walked up the granite steps taken, like everyone's granite steps, she'd learned, from Elizabeth Island quarries.

The entry hall was half of what it had once been, but it still had the full stairs. The living room was narrowed. Everything was heavy curtains and photographs and Catholic bric-a-brac.

Anna Rose called, "Come back here."

Past a wall that shut off what would have been the dining room, Carol came to what must always have been the whole kitchen. It had not been remodeled since the fifties. It was big and bright, and its windows looked out over other people's roofs to the tin reflection of the outer harbor. She didn't see any boats.

Anna Rose stood beside her stove. She wasn't much taller than the stove or the linoleum counters to either side. She wore her black tunic and black pants.

She said, "Sit down at my kitchen table."

Carol would just as soon have turned around and gone to work, but she sat on a chrome and red-plastic-seated chair beside the red enameled kitchen table.

Anna Rose sat down on a straight-backed wood chair. She was older than Carol, but not by all that much, and Carol felt like a girl visiting someone's mother.

Carol touched her long fingers along the painted-over chipping in the enamel at the edge of the table. It was a table like the one she and her father used to sit at. Before she could reach standing up, Carol had knelt on a chair to help him make hamburger patties, both pairs of their hands in the bowl. She'd done her homework there at the table while he smoked.

Anna Rose said, "I have called both of our United States senators. They are going to talk to me. Their staffs were expecting me to call. They will try to help. Also, you need something to drink. I have coffee and tea, and I have sherry for the priest, but we are too busy to drink that now."

Carol said, "Easy is going out so his crew can make money before the regulations take effect."

Anna Rose said, "Ignacio has both of his boats going out also. They call their crews, and they take their boats out. If they are already out, they come in so they can go out. You don't know, but you'll learn. We will get through this. We get through everything. Remember, Christ was with the fishermen first. Which is true, but I never say it to the senators until after they have done something for me."

There were no surprises left, but Carol felt as if it was only now sinking in. She said, "I don't think we're going to get through it this time."

Anna Rose said, "You know how I know it will be fine? Because the men called their crews and took the boats out. They think they have to do that, but you and I know they are better out of the way. I say, Good riddance."

Carol said, "This morning, Baxter Blume offered to buy Elizabeth Island's Best for one and a half times what we paid, and I turned them down." Carol could hardly believe she had turned them down, but she would turn them down again. It wasn't just a company; it was her. She was no longer the Beast. She didn't bury companies anymore, and she wasn't going to bury her own company. She couldn't fire her own people. Elizabeth had become her home, and she had to believe that as a businesswoman and as her father's daughter and finally as a CEO, she could make everything work.

Anna Rose said, "Of course you turned them down."

"I should have sold."

"You did right, Carol. Who cares about one and a half times some money on selling your own family?"

Carol had expected Anna Rose to realize it had been the wrong decision. She had hoped that Anna Rose would hate her and tell the rest of Elizabeth Island to hate her.

Carol said, "The fresh business was our margin. Without that, we'll run through all the cash reserves we have. If I shut it all down right now and fire-sale what I can gut, and throw in whatever we get for the toothfish, if it clears, maybe, maybe, I'll have a quarter of the total investment. With what the plant building would bring when nobody has to match the fat boys and there are no useful prospects, that might, in the best case, get us to half the total investment."

As if she hadn't heard a word, Anna Rose said, "Carol, you don't know tomorrow. I don't know tomorrow. That is why the men take the boats out as fast as they can and I call the politicians. To be ready for tomorrow."

Carol looked down at the green, smoke-swirled linoleum floor. She saw that Anna Rose wore black house slippers and black socks.

Carol spoke to the slippers. She said, "You and Buddy lost half your investment in two weeks. So did Dave Parks. So did Easy. Easy wanted me to sell. He thought I cared about my company more than I cared about him, and I did. We were together last night and this morning. Until he left."

Anna Rose said, "Carol," and would have gone on, but Carol shook her head.

"Hopefully you lose only half. Probably it's more. So will Annette Novato and Ben Garcia."

Carol bent over as if she were going to fall through the linoleum, and in one clumsy movement, she was on her knees before Anna Rose. She knelt by the chrome leg of her father's kitchen table and put her cheek onto Anna Rose's lap.

As soon as she knew Anna Rose would not push her away, Carol began to cry. She knew she was too big, but she put her bare arms around Anna Rose's heavy knees, and she cried for the second time in a day. She cried for everything and for never having had a lap to cry on.

Anna Rose smoothed Carol's hair and said, "Many people like Easy very much, and Easy said he liked you very much as soon as he first saw you, which it is not like Easy to say. Easy is a lonely man. That is why he fishes so well. Sometimes the good fishermen have big families, and the fish are how they afford their families. Sometimes the best fishermen have no families, because the fish are their family. But lonely does not always go on forever. People change."

Carol stopped crying. She felt her hair being stroked like a girl who has someone to love her after she's lost everything and deserved to lose it.

Anna Rose said, "You know how I know it will be fine? Because the fish are in the ocean. Ignacio and Easy are good fishermen, and they say there are fish. They say if they could get observers on their boats, it would be no question to anybody."

Carol heard that.

Something went off and she lifted her head. Baxter was not in the room; he would have been terrified of women crying and consoling, but he was not far outside. Carol didn't know where it was leading, but she was having a knee-jerk.

She said, "Observers?"

"Observers," Anna Rose said. "The fish are coming back slowly, but they are coming. Observers would see that. Without observers, we have to find another way. To you I can say, Fishes and loaves. I cannot say that to the senators right now, because they might think I don't insist they do their job. They might think someone else can take care of the fishermen. But observers are too expensive when the government has spent all its money on computers that can say when Easy and Buddy are lying about how much cod has to be thrown back. And do you know who is telling the computers what to say? Researchers who have gone out to catch fish themselves. And do you know who took those researchers out? The worst fishermen, the fishermen who couldn't get their own boats or who couldn't catch enough fish to keep the boat they got from their fathers, the fishermen everybody laughed about. They didn't know where the fish were, and they didn't know how to catch them. So the researchers told the computers, 'No fish.' And when the real fishermen and I and other wives tell the judge that we need real observers on real boats, the judge says we have done that and there's no money to do again what's already been done."

Carol said, "Observers." That was it. The government might not want to pay for observers, but Carol did, and she thought that she could. She also sensed something else, about the judge, but first things first. She said, "How much did the toothfish bring?"

"Oh, I see. You're back to work. Good. So for the toothfish, I got, we all of us got, a lot of us were calling, two million, one hundred and forty-five thousand dollars. In one day we got it. All of it is in the bank as money, by wire or by credit card, which Dave got the girl at the bank to help me with."

Carol stood up and said, "Thank you, for everything." Her voice was still thick from crying, but the pieces had fallen into place.

She cleared her throat of emotion so she could speak as happily and irreverently as Baxter. She said, "Also, do you know people at the Boston papers and television stations?"

Anna Rose stood up and spread her legs in a position of solid readiness and studied Carol. "You have a big *also*, don't you? Yes, I know all the newspaper and television people, the ones that can help, and they know me. We have had lots of practice together. The world has been trying to kill fishermen for a long time, and the way you keep fishermen alive is to make noise. What noise do you want?"

"Can I tell you in a little while, maybe an hour?" Carol had to change the judge's mind. She had two million dollars' worth of observers to do it, and she thought she could make the judge look good in the bargain.

"I will call and tell them to expect something."

Carol turned, and Anna Rose said, "Wait. I have done clean laundry for my grandson who is too tall to belong in our family but we love him just the same, and he is just your size. I think if you are going to be doing for the harbor, and doing it with judges and politicians, which otherwise why do you need papers and televisions, you would look more like one of us in blue jeans and a flannel shirt."

Anna Rose disappeared into a room off the kitchen and came back with the jeans and shirt. Carol stepped into the laundry room to change. She didn't need a mirror to tell her that the jeans and shirt fit well enough. She was glad to be in them.

She came out with her suit over her arm, and Anna Rose said, "Also, don't forget this is your home now, this island and this house, and you are in Taormina clothes."

Carol nodded gratefully. This was the loneliest day of her life, and she wasn't from fishing stock and she wasn't from this harbor, but she understood her work, and she was doing her best, and she thought she could pull this off, and something else for the judge came to her.

At the door, she turned back to Anna Rose and said, "So this injunction the judge ordered?"

Anna Rose said, "What?"

"Did the Wives have standing in the case?"

"Of course. We have standing in everything. It is what we do."

"Did you or anybody else bring up the lousy fishermen? Were they really lousy?"

"They were worse than lousy. They were barely fishermen. They came from here, and they were the funny line for every joke on the harbor. They did things nobody could believe. All they ever caught were those researchers, which was another joke until what has happened. Oh. I see. Nobody ever did bring up these joke fishermen. But now you want me to find out about them. Am I right? As grounds for a motion to have the judge suspend her injunction."

"Can you do it?" Carol asked.

"I know their names, and they are all in police records and in the harbormaster's logs. These are official jokes. We could have a television series. And you know what else? The Wives have a lawyer who has been working on this and works cheap but good and knows everything and can go as fast as we can get him the records, which is less than an hour, and in this case, with the injunction causing material this and material that, the motion has whatever you call it."

"Urgency."

"Urgency. Excuse me. I have to go to the telephone."

Carol went down the granite steps to the sidewalk and Mary, where she wasn't chipped, was as blue as the sky had been that day on Easy's boat.

⅄

Carol parked in the truck turnaround out from the old plant's loading bays. She admired Ben Garcia's ride. He had Brembos and a new set of eighteen-inch low-profiles. When she was ready, she took a breath and dialed Dave Parks on her cell.

Parks said, "Tell me something good."

"How close do we have to two million in ready cash with what Anna Rose dumped in yesterday?"

Parks said, "I beg your pardon." He said it agreeably; but he still said it. He said, "You sound ready to use our toothfish money in ways I can't imagine. Which could mean something good, if you aren't at an airport."

Carol laughed and said, "It's real. I think I can make this judge's decision work out, and we need that toothfish money for observers on the boats. The observers, and some theater if I can pull it off, are the bribe we offer the judge."

Parks said, "We have a full two million plus necessary operating money for a while. We haven't put anything out; it's all cash."

"Dave, I need a cashier's check for two million. I'm not sure who to make it out to right now, but I hope I need it soon, so let's get it immediately. Can you set that up, and I'll call you right back with a payee? Fifteen minutes."

"Two questions, Carol. Is your ticket one-way? And do you know it's Saturday at the bank?"

"Ask your friends at Elizabeth Savings and Loan how friendly they are to people who can deposit what we deposited yesterday."

"I'm pretty sure you're not at the airport. Does that make me sufficiently cautious?"

Carol could tell he was on board, even if he was in the dark for the moment. Parks was a good guy and a good businessman and a quick study. She said, "If we're going to buy back into the game, we're going to do it now."

"You never should have been an undertaker, Carol. You've got too much juice. Call me in fifteen for your cashier's check. Just don't call me irresponsible."

Parks sang that part, which was good to hear even if it wasn't his usual.

She said, "You're already having fun again."

"Is there a choice?"

Your Honor

Baxter was pissed that Carol had stiffed him, but it was not the end of the world. In some ways, he was proud of her. She knew she was making a shitty business decision, but she wanted that company and she was prepared to go down with it. Or not. Maybe she could pull something off.

Baxter had the kind of breakfast his wife no longer allowed him to eat at home. Then he called all sixteen members of the family to tell them he had irons in the fire. He did not get anybody working on discovering a stand-in for Carol's company. He thought that if something good didn't fall from the sky of its own accord in the next hour or so, he'd walk away like Carol had walked away but without consequences.

Then he saw a call from Carol coming in, which was very close to something falling from the sky. He didn't answer and let two more of her calls go by. He picked up the fourth.

"I changed my mind," she said.

He was eager, and he didn't pretend otherwise. He said,

"Carol. Perfect timing. We're at a standstill over here. It was my fault this morning. It was early. You were distracted. I could have handled it better. I'm delighted you called. How can I make it more comfortable for you? Do we have a deal? One and a half times your cost? I've forgotten about the sea bass completely. And truth be told, Carol, I want you to work with me. I've followed you at your fish plant, and you've done great. You may also be having more fun than I am. But just because I'm taking a backseat in the firm doesn't mean I don't have interesting deals of my own in the works, and I want you to come back and work with me on those deals. Real work, with participation. No more burials. I'm putting all my chips out here, Carol, because I think I can get to bed early if I offer my dopes over here the right box of chocolates, as you called it. Are we on? I wouldn't go this fast if I didn't know that you know all my bullshit. I can't tell you how glad I am you called."

"I'd like two times our cost."

He'd never underestimated Carol. She was dealing from weakness. So was he.

He said, "Oh, no. I can't. It's crazy. Holy shit, this. Holy shit, that. Blah, blah, blah." He enjoyed negotiating with adults who knew what they were doing. It was more fun, if not more profitable, than taking advantage of all the poor bastards who thought they knew.

"Okay," Baxter said. "You get two times your cost, but the clock is ticking, and if it ticks over, Carol, then life goes on and we never talked. Do we have our deal?"

"And I need you to get me in to see the judge for ten minutes."

"There's an *and* when I just gave you two times what you went in with two weeks ago? And why the judge? What does she have that you want? The judge smells like bullshit, Carol."

Carol had something on another burner. Not necessarily bad for Baxter, however. He didn't want to offer his belly to a knife Carol had behind her back, and he didn't put the judicious stabbing beyond Carol, but he felt that if he got a commitment from her it would be a real commitment, and then the judge, the knife, whatever else was on her stove wouldn't matter. If Carol was smart enough to lift some new sort of company right out of the ashes of this one, more power to her. Carol had tuned hoodlum cars in the back alleys of parts-plants Detroit. Carol had brains to go with her balls. Baxter waited for her to speak more about the judge, but he knew Carol was not going to elaborate until Baxter himself did some speaking; Carol had her back up.

He said, "And you want the judge today, I assume. Now. Is it really important enough to bring up before I deliver my box of chocolates? What for? You want to take a swing at her for pulling the rug out? That's not like you." Still nothing from Carol.

"No, you want to persuade her to reverse her decision. You're not passing the most basic smell test here, Carol, which is definitely not like you, but interesting. The thing is, every coastal district congressman for three hundred miles has already tried to persuade her and failed, and you don't have their weight. You are going to sell the company to me."

He waited for a response. Silence. Carol MacLean was blossoming. That was worth coming up here for all by itself.

He said, "Even if I find somebody who can get me through to the judge, I'm all day in the middle of trying to herd all these unhappy people who don't know business from backstroke into taking your company and giving me what I want. It shouldn't be difficult, but families are murky. It won't help to have to take calls from the judge and whoever guards her gate. I'm not going to mention to you that I'll have to ask favors to reach the judge.

But let's get straight on the real question. Am I right that you're selling?"

She said, "If talking to the judge buys you my company, your unhappy people get glad right away. When I start working with you, I'll make it a point to collect favors only you can dole out."

Baxter waited a moment as if considering before saying, "That's all? That's your best answer?"

"I'm selling," Carol said.

Baxter was quiet until she said it again, firmly. "I'm selling."

He said, "I'll get the judge," and hung up.

An American Picture

Carol sat in her car with her foot on the clutch and clicked up and down through six quick-throw gears. This would not be the last time she spoke to Baxter, but it would be the last time Baxter would trust her. She was sorry, but not that sorry. She was proud of herself. She was fighting for her company's life.

This was the plan: she would promise the judge two million dollars to pay for observers. Then she would call the fishing fleet into Elizabeth Harbor. The judge would show up at the harbor and make an announcement about the observers. She would change her decision again and let the fishermen fish. The judge would be someone who could make things work out, and she'd be a friend of the workingman and the ocean at the same time, on television. It was a perfect plan. It was a long shot.

Carol had been crossing lines since she left New York, and right now she felt as if they all added up to the line she'd just crossed with Baxter. Not a big line in most people's scheme of things, but it was critical if her company was going to have a chance.

Carol started her car long enough to lower her windows. The funk of low tide, which she had already learned to savor, flushed Baxter out of her head.

She called Anna Rose.

She said, "It's me."

Anna Rose said, "Of course it is. We got the police records. The harbormaster already had a file of copies of the pages of the logs that we need. He reads them when he needs cheering up. By now the lawyer is delivering. He had been ready to file a motion but didn't have good reasons. Also, for what good it will do, I have already talked to the congressman who matters, and I can talk again. From both senators, I have been called by the worker who goes to Harvard, the worker whose family knows the senator, the junior aide, and the middle aide. Next, either I get the senior aide or the senator. I have talked to the television and the papers, and they are ready when we have something. But Carol, everybody knows this judge. If you make her look bad, she will do things worse. She wants everybody to know she is in charge. If I were anybody who got nervous, I would get nervous about punching this judge. She is also running for governor. Did I already say that?"

Carol took a breath.

"I'm meeting the judge, and if your lawyer will fax just the records of those awful fishermen, I will talk to the judge about our motion."

"And then?

"I have two million dollars that she can give to the regulatory agencies to pay for observers. I'm going to let her be the arranger of a big offer of good-faith, good-cause, good-science money from historic Elizabeth Harbor."

Anna Rose was silent. The waiting, again. Carol could have been with Baxter.

Carol said, "No?"

"What is your no? You're going to do it anyway, and you should. It is a great idea and it's why we sold those toothfish. You knew we needed observers. Yes, Carol, but I'm trying to think what next. I am thinking we could still use a what next. She is running for governor."

Carol laid it out as fast as she could. The judge running for governor only gave it more leverage. This was the kind of horseshit Baxter, from the day he was born, could imagine, and imagine doing, and do before lunch.

"I want to see if Easy and Buddy will bring their boats, and as many other boats as they can, into Elizabeth Harbor. You and the Wives of the Sea meet them. And the judge. The papers and the television stations meet everybody. We make as much noise as we can, and we give the judge a way to make everybody happy. On television. She can put independent observers out on the water, which she can paint as controlled science for the environmentalists. For the fishermen . . ."

Anna Rose said, "For the fishermen, the judge can suspend her injunction, and that means we can still get fresh fish into our plant. Elizabeth Island's Best. Carol, you are saving your company, and you are saving my grandson his inheritance."

Now, Carol thought, they just had to make it work. She said, "If Easy and Buddy are right about the observers, we get a long-term suspension of the injunction and maybe in time full reversal of her opinion on the amendment."

"Easy and Buddy are right. But you see? You figured it out. I am not a bit surprised. And you got an appointment with the judge, which is a surprise. Only I have one suggestion to add and it is a great suggestion, because if we want to persuade the judge to change her mind, we have to go all-out. Have the boats come to Boston Harbor."

Carol had thought Elizabeth Harbor. Anna Rose went right to Boston Harbor. Carol wondered if Anna Rose and Baxter would like each other.

It was a long shot, but it was a shot. She almost dared to hope that they could save her company. She did not dare to hope that Easy might come back.

"No," Anna Rose said. "It's more. Once they get in the harbor, they all come to the *Constitution*. With this judge, it would be best if she could meet the boats there, with us. And the television. She will want that. She is going to run for governor."

"What's the *Constitution*?"

"Carol. Are you first generation? It is your oldest Navy ship. Very famous. If the Coast Guard tries to keep our boats away, that is a good American picture for every evening news. If the boats can come all the way to the *Constitution*, that is a better American picture. I will get our Wives and extra wives, and we will wait for our fishermen. Do you think the judge will agree to the observers? I think she will. The boats that are far out, you won't get them, but the boats that are not so far, and with them coming north and south, as well as west, full speed and in calm sea, in three, four hours you have got a full harbor, and I mean a full Boston Harbor. How soon do you see her?"

Baxter would never want to fail when he'd said he would "make some calls." But that might sound vague to Anna Rose, so Carol asked her own question. "Does Buddy have a phone on his boat? I'd better start trying to bring the boats in."

"You call Easy, too. Because listen, Carol. In my grandfather's time and before, in Italy, in Sicily, sometimes fishermen died. And many times it was a storm, and sometimes it was that a fisherman wanted to die. A man goes out on purpose where he shouldn't, and either he dies like he thinks he wants or God brings him back. If women want to die, they choose the wrong man. Men and women, it never changes. You hear me, Carol? Easy loves you. Everybody on the harbor knows, and he is a good man. If you don't get him on the phone, tell me and I'll use the radio. Then the whole fleet can hear, and he will decide to answer the phone after all."

Carol said, "Thank you," and took down both numbers Anna Rose gave her, Buddy's and Easy's.

She had to put the fishermen and their boats in motion before she talked to the judge, and if the boats were going to arrive in time, she had to get them started now. She had to have faith that Baxter would get her in to the judge. She didn't think anymore about what she was doing with Baxter's faith in her. She wondered if, once she reached the judge, the judge would go along. The judge had made a big decision with the injunction, and made it publicly. If the judge shut Carol down and the boats were already headed for Boston Harbor . . . Well, Carol thought, she didn't have a choice.

She called Buddy, and told him what was happening. He said, "Let me call you some other boats. Everybody's on the water. Everybody's on the radio, dying over the amendment. Yeah. Good for you, Carol. I'll get 'em moving."

"I was hoping you'd call Easy," she said.

She hung up, and with the smell of the harbor, with the understanding that Buddy had been speaking from his boat, Carol felt that she was on the water herself. Strangely, she didn't feel sick.

She studied her plant out the windshield. She knew, better than her dad, about half-assed outfits that struggled and died competing with factories that had proper systems and sufficient scale. She was glad she'd gotten the Cyclone fence pulled.

She wasn't going to call Easy. Buddy was going to call him. Carol wanted to hear Easy's voice, but she didn't have any illusions that he would suddenly want her back. When he got on the elevator to leave her, he knew that she cared more for her company than for anything that mattered to him. If she could find a way to keep her company and keep Easy fishing out of Elizabeth Harbor, she would do that and try not to want more.

He could help. She called him for that. She would tell him it was for the harbor and for his boat, and for the investors, and the town, for the people who would work in the plant.

She dialed his number, and before she spoke, he said, "Hi, Carol."

She remembered how much she loved his voice. She wanted to be in her plant, and him to be working his boat out of the harbor, and every night that he was in port, they could touch each other. But she couldn't say these things.

Carol didn't recognize her own voice, and she spoke even faster than she'd spoken to Anna Rose. "Buddy's going to call you. I think we may be able to get the injunction suspended and observers on the boats. A lawyer is filing a motion right now, about the terrible fishermen who drove the boats out with researchers to see what was caught. And I'm going to offer the judge the toothfish money to pay for real observers going out with real fishermen, and I'm also trying to make news with your guys' boats and with Anna Rose's Wives. Buddy will tell you. It's all the boats coming to Boston Harbor. Right now. Please come."

He said, "Carol." He sounded as if he wanted to say more. But he didn't.

Instead, she said, "If we get the amendment suspended, could you still fish out of the harbor and bring your fresh catch to us?"

He said, "Carol," and she didn't dare wait for more. She couldn't bear to hear him say no.

She said, "I think this can work. I should hang up. I'm sorry. Buddy will call and tell you. Please, Easy. Come to Boston Harbor, and then if we make it work, come home to Elizabeth Harbor."

She hung up and put her head down on the steering wheel and concentrated on the touch of his voice, and the touch ran away from her. She said aloud to her steering column, "It's a nice little plant. Good for me."

She got Parks and Annette in Parks's office and told them about the judge and the boats and the Wives and the media and the observers and the check and the motion to suspend the injuction. Then she said, "Let's make that check out to the Fund for Observers of Northeast Fisheries. Does that sound workable? Have we got the check? If things don't pan out, can we tear it up?"

Annette said, "Why do we have to do it so fast?"

"I'm not sure we do; maybe we don't, but it feels like we have momentum, and I'm counting on getting in to see the judge. Like it or not, wheels are rolling."

Parks said, "Creedence. Remember Creedence?" He hummed a few lines.

"You're feeling good, Dave."

"I'm getting there."

"And you have the check."

"We've got a check waiting for a payee, and we've also got a plant ready to run on Monday morning. Where are you?"

"Where do you think I am?"

"I think you're out off the loading dock, in blue jeans and a flannel shirt."

"I'll call you as soon as I know I can use the check. Thanks, Dave."

She hung up and held the phone in her lap and waited for Baxter. He would come through quickly, because he was in a hurry, too. He might have to give away something he liked, but he assumed he was getting something he wanted. He must have guessed she was doing a deal. In any case, there was no going back. Carol would have to keep lying, and lying better, and she was ready for it.

She was sure that the boats, a lot of them, were on their way to Boston Harbor, and she believed she was right to be sure. She didn't know whether Easy was coming.

Lying

It had not been a quarter of an hour since Baxter talked to Carol, and he knew she was sitting with the phone in hand, waiting to hear from him, and she let it go four rings. It was adolescent courtship that drove the business, still.

Fifth ring. A quarter of an hour ago, he had felt she was just about there as a killer, even if only a nice, thoughtful killer. Now, he had a strong sense that he would not want Carol MacLean to pack his parachute.

She picked up on the sixth ring, and Baxter said, "She'll see you in an hour and a half. For ten minutes. What an asshole. Be glad it's only ten minutes. But the guys on the other team in the room here at the Four Seasons, they all knew who she was, very impressed. She's running for something."

"I'm impressed, too, Baxter. Thank you."

Murderer. No question. He was proud to take credit.

He said, "Bullshit. Why do you want to see her, Carol?"

"I want to look her in the eye and tell her what she's doing to a way of life."

"Also bullshit. You want to turn her around, and you think you can. She's a big shot, Carol, and she's made a public decision. She doesn't turn around. I told you, she's running for something."

Baxter heard that hopelessly hopeful speech, a speech best given to the mirror, and he knew as sure as God created gullible people that he was the murderee.

"All right, I do want to turn her around. Of course I do. I also know as well as you that she's not going to turn around for me or anyone else. All I really want in a practical way is to try, to at least have made the effort. It's not business. It's personal, and I ought to know better."

Baxter expected her to say she was doing it for the fisherman she'd thrown over. He was glad she'd decided to leave all that unsaid. But after a calculated pause, she said, "I want to be able to tell Easy Parsons, the fisherman you met, that I did all I could to keep him here, to keep him fishing here. I wouldn't expect you to pay much attention to that. I'm afraid Easy won't either."

Baxter lifted his shirt so her knife could go in cleanly. He pointed up under his ribs on the left side. He said, "I have your judge, and you'll get her, but I do need something from you that I can offer to all these guys. I wish they were all guys. Can I tell them we have a deal?"

He didn't need to hear the answer, though he was interested in what her phrasing would be. You played these things out. And he liked Carol. He'd done nice things in his life, but not many quite like this. It felt good. Not a feeling he was going to indulge again anytime soon.

She said, "Baxter, I won't formally commit to anything until I've seen the judge." Baxter supposed she really was in love, even if it was over. And if it had her by the throat, so be it. Nothing indictable in that. He didn't think there'd been enough of it in Carol's life. She said, "I won't formally commit until I've made my try. It's a little thing, but I am going to see my judge. Then we talk about the terms of my employment with you."

"I want your word that I get to buy your company. No contract implied. I just want your personal promise."

"Then, yes. Of course. You have it. I promise."

Baxter was not sure how Carol expected to turn the judge. But he knew that her company was a good thing for her and probably for her town. She'd gotten her hands a little dirty. Who was he to cast stones?

"I'm going to patch you in to an intern who has the directions to her house."

"Thank you, Baxter."

"You're welcome. Thank you. Everybody's happy. We'll talk next week."

Between this chat with Carol and the one fifteen minutes ago, Baxter had lost the box of chocolates he'd promised and with it the nice little piece he could have used. Oh well, as the kids would say.

To the Judge

Dave was sitting in his office when Carol came in with Ben Garcia. Instead of a blue suit, Carol was wearing the jeans and the flannel shirt. She looked like she'd been wearing them all her life. Blue-collar woman, Dave thought. Looked good. Ben, on the other hand, was going with new pressed jeans and a pressed long-sleeve shirt. He was revved up. Carol looked revved up herself.

She said, "Ben's going to drive me to the judge's in his car. Finally, I have a reason to ask him for a ride."

That sounded like fun to Dave, and they looked like they knew it. It was all Dave could do not to ask if he couldn't come out to play with them.

Carol said, "If she tells me to get lost, I'll hide under the bed until the fishermen and the papers and TV forget the whole thing."

Dave considered the jeans. They definitely worked for a visit to the judge. A blue-collar message.

Carol picked up on him sorting the jeans and said, "I think they work."

"I agree," Dave said and handed her the cashier's check and tried not to look like the puppy left home. He said, "Knock 'em dead, Carol."

She looked at him and said, "Oh, come on."

He said, "Far out," and pulled off his tie, kicked off his loafers, laced up his plant sneakers.

He sat in the tiny backseat, ass almost to the floor, and knew the discomfort would only get worse, and didn't care, yet. Great car. He could feel the snarl of the exhaust vibrate his cheeks. He held the directions to the judge's house and called out turns once they got on small roads. On those roads, Ben started some serious driving, and Dave had to say, "Let's don't get busted."

Carol said, "The hell with the cops. We have an appointment with the judge."

Where had Carol been all his business life? Dave wondered. Maybe she was wondering where she had been herself.

Everybody knew where the judge had been. She had a real colonial name, and she'd been schooled just right and married just right and mothered just right and even divorced just right. Dave had seen her on television. She was petite and stern, pretty and smart as hell. Also patrician as hell, which she had to fight to get the Southie vote and the fish vote. Her house was a handsome colonial, if bigger than what the early relatives ever had, and it was blue-blood deep in stone walls and meadows and orchards.

The driveway turnaround was also big, and Dave would have had Ben park off to the side with the two Jaguars, though at a respectful distance from them.

Leave It Running

Since Carol had seen the morning paper in the hotel hallway, risk had been increasing around her and inside her like the temperature in a boiler as it came on line.

So instead of enjoying the ride in Ben's car, she used the time to focus. Baxter could promote off the cuff anywhere about anything, but Carol, once she'd gotten a sense of things on a project, had always broken down the elements and tried to understand how they would play out, in what order and with what resistance and results. She didn't like to go naked.

She was on her way to the judge. She was wearing the blue jeans Anna Rose had given her. She had a check for two million dollars, and the records and logs of the pathetic fishermen who supposedly helped the researchers catch fish in order to calculate the presence and viability of species. The lawyer had already gotten a motion to the judge's office and to wherever else it had to go. And all of the New England fishing fleet within reach was heading to Boston Harbor, and the media frenzy Anna Rose had called in.

Carol didn't know if getting the injunction suspended would bring Easy back to her, but if she didn't get it suspended, for sure he would take his boat somewhere too far away, which was no part of what she was selling the judge.

They came in the driveway and up to the house, and Carol was tempted to park off to the side of the Jaguars. Instead she said, "Stop right in the middle, Ben." Which Ben did, and she said, "Leave it running."

Even while just idling, Ben's car made a sound that was not polite in the judge's driveway. Carol loved the sound and loved it in front of the judge's house.

From the back seat, Dave said, "Are you sure?"

No, she wasn't sure, but she turned around and smiled.

And Dave, nodding at the exhaust, smiled despite himself.

Carol watched the front door of the judge's house, and when it opened, it opened too fast, and the judge, as if there was no walking involved, appeared on the front steps like a god. She was wearing an expensive version of the suit Carol usually wore. Today, however, Carol was wearing the jeans Anna Rose had lent her. She was also holding a cashier's check for two million dollars at her side.

She got out of the car and walked toward the house quickly but not apologetically. She walked just fast enough to say, respectfully, we're equals. Ben came with her.

The judge stood with her hands on her hips, and up there at the top of her steps, she didn't look as short as she really was. She also didn't look impressed that Carol was taller still.

She said, "I promised somebody that I'd give you ten minutes to tell me why I should suspend my injunction to restrict commercial fishing. I'm not going to give you ten minutes. I've heard every argument too many times to count, so I'm giving you thirty seconds. What have you got?"

Carol said, "There is a need to put responsible observers on fishing boats driven by capable fishermen. Earlier today, your office got a motion to suspend the injunction."

"I'm not impressed yet. Research observers have already been taking boats out to fish. That's how we know the fish are gone. You've filed a pointless motion. Your thirty seconds are up."

Carol said, "The fishermen taking those research observers out to fish were the worst fishermen in New England. Never in a hundred years could they have found fish, and if they'd found them, they couldn't have caught them if the fish were jumping into the hold."

The judge was already turning around toward her door, but she stopped when Carol held out the police records and harbor logs. The judge said, "For this, you get another thirty seconds."

The judge took the sheets and glanced and glanced again and read more closely. She smiled. She said, "I'm sympathetic to your cause, but I've made my decision, and I stand by it. This is how the law works. It's unseemly for a judge to flip back and forth and back again. It makes her look weak and the law look weak, and I would feel that way even if I weren't running for governor. And if I tried to find money to do observers all over again with better fishermen than these, people would line up to accuse me for every reason under the sun. I'm sorry."

Carol wished Baxter were here. He'd be amused, maybe even impressed, at how this was actually playing out the way it was supposed to play out. There was no guarantee it would continue to play out, but Carol felt surprisingly calm.

She held the check up so the judge could see it without having to take it.

The judge nodded and said, again, "Two million dollars doesn't buy cotton candy at the county fair, but it's a meaningful gesture. And it's not enough for me to change my mind. I'm sorry."

The judge handed back the records and logs.

Carol took the sheets and said, "As we speak, all of the New England fishing fleet within reach is heading into Boston Harbor. Every television station and newspaper will be waiting for them at the *Constitution*. Local and regional, and you'd have to think there'll be images for national exposure."

Ben said, "The USS *Constitution*."

The judge nodded to Ben and then turned back to Carol and said, "So what?"

"You're running for governor."

Carol thought that would be the last card she needed to play, but the judge said, "What difference does the fishing fleet make at this point? They'll have a nice photo opportunity, but I've already lost those votes."

Baxter would have known all along that Carol would have to play the last card. She played it. She said, "As well as the boats, the media is also waiting for you. They are expecting you in particular. If you don't show up for blue-collar heroes in Boston Harbor, you're too good for them. You're the rich candidate with blue blood who doesn't give a damn, and you lose, at a minimum, every working class vote in the state. Which would mean you are no longer a candidate for anything. If you do show up and say that you're prepared to suspend the injunction, then you're a woman who has the courage to change her mind given good enough reason. What's more, you're a woman with important family background who is also a stand-up woman of the people. And you've got the best campaign coverage and imagery maybe in history. You're governor."

"You told the fishermen and the media to expect me?"

"I had help getting the word out."

"So the real reason I'm suspending my injunction is that . . ."

Carol said, "The motion goes persuasively to the heart of the injunction's reasoning. The proof that the fish are gone is fundamentally flawed. And the matter of the injunction, shutting down the entire northeast fishery, or not, is urgent."

"What's your name, again?"

"Carol MacLean."

"I've never heard of you. And now I have to make some calls to check on your motion."

Carol said, "It's the Wives of the Sea."

The judge said, "Of course it is," and went in the house, shutting the door behind her.

Glory

Dave watched as Carol and Ben walked back to the car. It was only when Ben got in the driver's seat that Dave realized the judge, if she was coming, would want to come in Ben's car. Carol knew. She opened the other back door from where Dave sat and put a foot in and said, "Are we friends, Dave?"

He said, "If we aren't, it looks like we will be," and she angled and squeezed herself in beside him and closed that door. Then they sat, not more than a few minutes, but it felt like more. Dave said, "Do we know?"

Carol shook her head and handed the check up to Ben and said, "If she comes, give her this. No need to say anything." They sat another minute, and Carol said up to Ben, "Touch it once, Ben," and Ben did, and the car made its muscle noise.

Dave giggled and Carol said, "Get a grip, Dave."

And the judge came out and closed her front door behind her. She was wearing old khaki pants and high rubber mud-season boots and a faded checked shirt with the sleeves rolled up. It was an outfit probably for working with the special plants she didn't let the gardeners get near, but she looked real, and besides the rest, she had on a Red Sox hat that looked like it had been to twenty seasons of games. She came straight to Ben's car and got in the front passenger side door that Carol had left open and said, "Kick it, Ben."

They got to the highway, and a state police escort met them, and the judge, to her further credit, pushed a fist at the windshield. Ben, capable in all the important languages, stood on it. The officer went to flashers and dared Ben to keep up. Ben, first and only words on the drive, said, "Who's he think he's kidding?" Vibrations got to a level suggestive of breaking the sound barrier, but Dave was no way going to whimper. Carol, back of her head on the roof, was looking over Ben's shoulder, and Dave could only think she was checking to be sure Ben had it to the metal as she gave the judge additional details on the observers and Elizabeth Harbor and the old plant renewal.

They slowed when they wound into the maze of Charlestown, across the harbor from Boston. When they reached the harbor, the judge had Ben stop short of the Wives and the TV trucks and what looked like a volunteer crowd that was growing by the minute.

The last seconds waiting to get out of an agony squeeze inside a car are always the worst. And while Dave had assumed the judge would want to walk in through the crowd, now he figured out that she had to wait for somebody to find her if there was going to be the shot of her getting out of Ben's car. Dave should have been worried about Carol, but as soon as he could punch the seat back in front of him and dive out, he punched and dove. He looked back, and Carol was already out. She hadn't waited for him either.

Now the judge waved Carol and Ben up to do the crowd walk with her. Dave stayed close enough behind to watch Carol. Maybe she'd need a hand, but mostly he was a fan at a good game, and Carol was a late-in-life rookie burning up the league. She was tall, confident, flannel shirt, red hair frizzed, leading the judge into the Wives of the Sea while letting it seem the judge was leading. Dave admired the hell out of Carol.

Now Carol bent down like the right-hand political consultant, and the judge was listening, and now Carol was back up tall and waving and calling something into the Wives, and the Wives parted for some bumping progress through them. It was too low to see what it was, but it was moving through on a course for Carol. Carol's free hand was on the judge's shoulder. Dave could hardly believe how good Carol was.

It was Anna Rose Taormina coming through. TV cameras closing in from everywhere. Anna Rose hugging Carol and then hugging the judge, and the judge, a slight woman but a politician and an old-school Yankee to boot, hugging back to beat the band.

Carol started to step out of the picture, not easy in the corral of television equipment, but the judge turned back quick to get a hug from Carol, including a tiptoe kiss on the cheek. Dave froze the moment just long enough to tell himself he'd been smarter than Lazarus to sign on with Carol MacLean.

Anna Rose led the judge on into the crowd of Wives and news groups and the more and more onlookers.

Carol got Ben's hand and led him off to the side. When Dave caught up, Carol raised Ben's hand like for a champ, and Dave grabbed Ben's other hand and raised that one. Ben grinned like a champ. The judge would go home with her regular driver in a limo or whatever, but Ben had already had a day.

They worked toward the side of the crowd and in the general direction of the harbor. Carol pointed ahead at the three high white masts.

"What's that?"

Ben and Dave said at the same time, "The *Constitution*," like maybe Carol had been revealed as a Commie spy.

With that, they had to push to keep up with her until they got to where they could see the ship itself, with its black hull and its white stripe windowed for cannons, and the masts soaring.

Carol stopped and said, "That's it."

No sobbing, but she was damp in her eyes, and in fact it was a weepingly beautiful ship, how it looked and what it meant.

Then Carol said, "Oh, my god," and grabbed Dave's arm, and the three of them registered what was beyond the *Constitution*.

Crowding the harbor were boats—fishing boats: big ones, bigger ones, small and smaller ones. The water out there beyond the eighteenth-century three-masted warship was all but solid with today's boats that did work as ancient as war, and the guys on those boats must have learned that the judge had arrived, because a cacophony of horns lifted from the boats in a clanging howl that so shook the air that the towers of downtown Boston wavered like a mirage.

Ben, kid from El Salvador, said, "This is America." He was crying and Dave was not far from it.

Carol said, "It is."

Ben said, "It is people standing up and trying, everybody, and everybody a chance. That's why everybody ever came here and still comes."

There was the static barking of a public-address system, and they could look across a slip from the *Constitution* to where somebody, Anna Rose and her Wives, had set up a little stand and a microphone. The judge was ready to go.

Dave said, "You don't want to be over there?"

"Let her have it. People will know about us when it's time."

The judge, facing the cameras and the Wives and the crowd, said, pretty clear for a loudspeaker outdoors, "My office has just received a motion to suspend the injunction I recently issued, an injunction that all but shuts down the commercial New England fisheries. I didn't issue that injunction lightly. Fishing is in New England's bones; historically, it may in fact be New England's bones. As a New Englander from head to toe, fishing is certainly in my bones." The judge stopped and took a breath and looked over her audience. They were not, even with all the news people, a glamorous bunch. But everybody was paying serious attention, and when the judge took her breath, the attention got more serious.

"I studied and weighed all the data and all the arguments, and as much as I agonized over the implications for people and harbors and history and even our New England soul, I finally didn't feel I had any choice but to issue the injunction. We are the stewards of our ocean and the fish that live in it. Having issued the injunction, I am not inclined to suspend it immediately. That's how the law works, and it's also how I work. I am, in fact, inclined to be adversarial to any motion to suspend. The motion that came in today, however, calls into serious question the fundamental data on which I made my decision. That's a problem for me and it's a problem in the law. A motion to suspend, if it's to have any chance of success, must present compelling reasons. The motion I received today presents compelling reasons, and it also suggests sound methods for acquiring more trustworthy data on our fish stocks. There is a reasonable possibility that our stocks are not as bad as suspected and that with far less draconian regulations than proposed in the injunction, fishing could continue off our shores. Even with this encouraging news, however, I worry that the expense of opening this matter up to further study would be prohibitive in these financially uncertain times. Happily, all but miraculously, money has come from the fishing community of Elizabeth Harbor to pay for the further study. It's not enough money—there never is enough money—but it's a meaningful start, and it has convinced me that I have another decision to announce. I'm here now to make that announcement, but first I want to tell the men and women behind me, the fishermen who have come in today hoping to mark another splendid chapter in the history of our great harbor."

The stations must have been broadcasting out so the boats could pick it up, because all the horns had gone quiet.

The judge turned around to face the harbor and the boats. In the quiet, you would have thought the boats themselves were listening. The judge stood still, letting the moment be the moment. The boats waited. Dave waited. Carol and Ben waited. A politician, Dave thought, but sometimes you needed them.

The judge raised both arms. Tiny woman, but both arms went up, and from Boston to Tokyo, you knew it was a touchdown, and the boats, the horns, erupted, lifting the harbor.

Painter

Carol searched for Easy's boat. She searched by quadrants, going from right to left. She didn't know what she'd do if she saw his boat, but she needed to know where it was. If it was here, and if that was close as she could get to him, she needed to know she was at least that close. She didn't see it. The *Beauty*. She went back from left to right. The only boats she could distinguish were small ones coming in close, somebody in a rubber rowboat, kayaks, a Windsurfer.

Dave and Ben were moving around to where everybody was, and Carol started to follow them and then worried it would be harder to pick out Easy's boat if she were in the crowd. She walked out farther on the pier. She was alone. She started searching back right to left. She was short of breath and she had to squeeze her hands into fists, to stay focused in her search. She heard a shout about beauty and paid no attention. She ignored all the sounds drifting from the crowd. Carol was looking. She gazed above the small boats and the oddities to search among the big boats farther out. She realized that she would not recognize Easy's boat from so far away, if he'd even come. He had to be out fishing for his crew every minute before the regulations took effect.

She heard it again, and she knew the voice, and it was nearby. "Beauty."

Right here below her, it was Easy in the rubber rowboat, grinning. Carol's breath got shorter, and Easy said, in a pleased-with-himself voice, "I rowed."

Carol didn't feel herself sinking down, but she was on her knees, just like she'd been when he first came to her, when she was an undertaker expecting her own company and had instead found herself buried with all the men and women she'd been burying for years and years.

Easy laughed and said, "Take the painter," and because of the instant in which she looked around for somebody with a paintbrush, she almost missed catching the rope he tossed up to her. She did catch it, and she laughed herself and held that rope for dear life.

She held it until Easy boosted himself up onto the dock beside her. He tied the rope to something and took hold of her shoulders and stood her up.

He said, "You did it," and he was still grinning like he had everything just right. "I can fish out of Elizabeth Harbor and bring my fresh catch to you." Then he let go of her shoulders, and she didn't know whether to tell him that he shouldn't let go, that he should hold her, so she reached around and hugged him herself. She smelled him, his sweat and the sea. He'd rowed in from the *Beauty*. She watched his face as he grinned again and then he had his arms around her, and he kissed her like he was supposed to do and she kissed him of course, and out over the harbor, the horns were going again. Which would have been more than enough for Carol, enough for anybody. Except then Easy leaned back, just a bit, and looked at her, and saw her.

Acknowledgments

Particular thanks to Joe Regal, Jon Karp, Emily Graff, Sallie Bingham, and Justin Colin.

A legion of people read and contributed to one or more of the forest of drafts *Beauty* went through. If I do not name all of those people here, I thank them just the same, a lot, and I beg them to understand their own names among these few souls whose insistence I can't shake: Ted Buswick, George Stalk, Ron MacLean, David Rosen, and Jack Parsons.

About the Author

Frederick Dillen was born in New York City's Greenwich Village and raised in a New Hampshire boarding school. A graduate of Stanford University, Dillen worked odd jobs from Lahaina to Taos and New York to Los Angeles, managing a hotel and running a fake ranch, carrying plates and shilling for business. His short fiction has appeared in literary quarterlies and *Prize Stories: The O. Henry Awards*. His first novel, *Hero,* was named Best First Novel of 1994 by the *Dictionary of Literary Biography*. His second novel, *Fool,* was honored by Nancy Pearl as a "Book Lust Rediscoveries" selection in 2012. Dillen and his wife, the actress and playwright Leslie Dillen, are the parents of two grown daughters and live in New Mexico with a yellow dog named Lucy.